TIME OF MY LIFE

MARY FRAME

Summary

Today is the worst day of Jane Stewart's life. And she's reliving it over and over (and over and over) again.

She's late to the same make-or-break meeting.
    She's fired from the same soul-crushing job.
    And—the cherry on top—she's dumped by the same lying, selfish dirtbag.

But no matter how many times she relives the same disasters and no matter what she tries to change them, it all ends in the same abysmal mess. Because, apparently, being stuck in a time loop on the worst day of her life hasn't cured her crippling social anxiety. Go figure.

The one bright spot? Her long-time crush wants to be more than friends . . . if only she can get them past their first date. And so her happily ever is doomed before it can even begin unless she can find a way to save her job, her heart, and, oh yeah, the space-time continuum.

To Dave Pijuan, a.k.a. O-Pijuan-Kenobi.
Thank you for being a wonderful cubicle mate, friend, and the best
melon picker ever.
You will be missed.

Chapter One

Belching. Someone is belching. Ugh, why is it so loud?

I roll over, pulling a pillow over my head. Pounding bass vibrates into my skull, shaking the walls. My pillow is not an effective barrier.

What is that?

Did he say hocus-pocus?

Is someone in my apartment? They broke in just to pass gas and play music at excessive levels?

Is it my alarm? *Oh no, it's Monday.*

I jerk up, already reaching for my phone to kill the noise, plucking it from the charging cord.

Wakefulness weaves its fingers through my sleepy mind. My heart thumps along with the music.

I stare at the blank screen. I barely slept last night. It took me forever to fall asleep, worrying over my meeting today, trying to think through every potential response and outcome. My dreams were full of every-thing that might possibly go wrong, from missing my notes to arriving late to showing up naked.

The memories fade as reality rushes in to take its place.

My phone is dead.

"That's not my alarm. My alarm didn't go off," I croak to the empty room.

The music is still thumping.

I stare at the dark phone screen. I always leave it charging to avoid this exact scenario.

"Oh, no. No no no no no." I rush out of bed, forgetting the cell phone mystery, skidding into the kitchen to stare at the clock on the oven.

It's nearly eight.

"This isn't possible."

Someone bangs on the door. Maybe the world is ending. That would be good. If there's some kind of disaster situation—a building fire, a tsunami incoming, aliens invading the planet, maybe—that would be the perfect excuse for being late for the most important meeting of my existence.

I swing open the door, but no one's there.

"Hugo! Come on, man, it can't be that bad."

I peek around my doorjamb. I don't want anyone to witness me in this state, no makeup, my hair a dark mass of chaos, not to mention the bright blue ducky pajamas, a gift from my sister, Eloise. But I can't help staying to witness . . . whatever this is.

A portly middle-aged man with thinning hair in a

bright red robe stands in front of the door next to mine. I don't know his name, only that he resides in the apartment across the hall from mine.

I generally avert my gaze to avoid small talk when I pass any of the other residents in my building, so I don't know much about any of them. Based on the masculine laughter—and other noises that sometimes penetrate the thin walls—I know my next-door neighbor is gay. But that's as far as it goes. I'm not good at small talk. Or any talk.

But now I unwittingly know my next-door neighbor's name.

Hugo.

It's fitting, considering his huge size. He's a goliath of a man, wide and tall. Body builder maybe. Football player. Possible assassin. Fearful, by all accounts. Except in his choice in music. While loud and pounding, "sparkle me" rapped over and over doesn't exactly inspire fear.

As the music hammers through the air with no response to the knocking, red-robe man pounds harder.

"It's Monday! I have a call in thirty minutes. Help me out here, huh?"

Monday. Meeting.

Oh, crap.

I slam the door and rush to the bathroom, racing through my morning ablutions, pitching my ducky pajamas into the hamper. No time for anything more than peeing and scrambling into the clothes I set out the night before, a sensible pale pink blouse and slimming black slacks. I toss a small bag of makeup into my briefcase on top of my proposal. Then I'm out the door, running to the BART station on the corner to catch the next train.

I barely make it in time, the doors shutting behind me as I squish in between a redheaded woman in a hot pink T-shirt and bright yellow pants and a man in an Armani suit on his cell phone, one of his hands clutching the pole in the center of the car.

Once the train is in motion, I grab my phone from my bag and hold down the power button. Maybe it needs a reset or something. If I can call the office, let them know I'm going to be late, make some excuse, maybe I won't have a panic attack on the train surrounded on all sides by strangers.

I shake my head and take a breath.

Focus, Jane. Phone. Work. Important meeting. But thinking about the upcoming meeting doesn't calm me. Instead, my heart races, my stomach twists into knots, black spots crowd the corners of my eyes, and my hands shake.

I breathe and stare at my phone until my vision clears and I can focus on pressing the power button down. It's not working. I take a deep, calming breath— and choke on the fumes from the cologne of the businessman next to me, earning me dirty looks from the rest of the passengers.

"Sorry," I cough into my hand.

I spend the rest of the train ride using a compact to try and fix my face and hair, but in the cramped train car it's an exercise in futility. Business man is on the phone the entire time, yelling about assets and liabilities and bitcoins, all while waving his free hand and smacking into my elbow while I'm attempting to put mascara on. I end up swiping a thick line of black under my cheek and poking myself in the eye three times. Finally, I give up.

The train jerks to a stop, forcing me to grab on to the pole under business man's hand and . . . ick. There's something on there. It's wet. I lift my hand. And it's brown.

Please, universe, let that be chocolate.

I sprint through the train station and up the stairs, wincing at the waft of sewer stench as I reach the street, dodging people and holding my dirty hand away from my body. I have nowhere to wipe it. Ugh. Why is my nicest, most professional blouse also pale pink?

Mother. That's why.

The office is a block from the station and I jog down the cracked sidewalk, my hair working itself into a truly remarkable frizzed-out halo surrounding my head. Of course I forgot to grab a hair clip.

When the glass-front entrance of the building comes into view, I nearly sob in relief. Almost there.

I've worked with Blue Wave Marketing for nearly four years. This meeting is going to determine whether I can be a senior marketer. It's what I've been working toward, handling my own accounts, running my own campaigns. I can't let one broken phone ruin everything.

I'm ten minutes late. What if they use this as a reason to reject my proposal? What if they decide they can't have a senior marketer who arrives late to important meetings? What if they laugh at me and call me a ridiculous waste of space? What if—

Stop it, Jane.

I push through the front door and immediately get a disgusted look from Hannah, the front desk executive. She flips a sleek length of blonde hair behind her shoulder and avoids my eyes.

Blue Wave is all about giving people advanced titles, and "receptionist" is much too demeaning. So front desk executive it is.

The entire office space exemplifies feng shui, open, airy, light, except for a cramped coffee station in the back that's cluttered with ten different espresso machines Brandon keeps ordering for reasons I still don't understand. There are two hallways on either side of the employee area, one that leads to a storeroom and bathroom, and on the other side, the conference room where I'm sure management is waiting for me.

Directly behind Hannah, all of the employees are spread out, no cubicles, all open space with individual desks. Even the team leaders sit among the rest of the crew because they believe in putting everyone on equal footing, regardless of title.

I'm not a junior marketer, I'm a "student" marketer. Because according to Blade, we are all learning. It's crap, but whatever.

"Hannah, please." I don't want to beg, but I have

no other choice. "Can you tell the team that I'm here and I'll be in shortly?"

She purses her enhanced lips, nose wrinkling in disdain.

Oh no, does my hand . . . smell? I sniff the brown gook and she glares at me like I've started licking the desk in front of her.

"I'm not your secretary. Tell them yourself."

Hannah has never been my biggest fan, but she's been especially rude for the past few months. I've racked my brain to figure out what I did, what stupid thing I might have said, and while there are many options, I still don't know what her deal is and I haven't asked. I hate confrontation with anyone, but with Hannah, who's naturally aggressive? I would rather rub naked against splintered wood.

Presley, another student marketer who has only been here a few months, pipes up from behind her. "I got it, Jane. You look like you need a sec."

Relief and nerves make my voice quiver. "Thank you, Presley."

She nods and strides away toward the hall to the conference room, her dark ponytail swinging behind her.

In the bullpen, Mark is tossing a stress ball back and forth with Brandon, brainstorming ideas for a campaign. He catches my eye and gives me a wink.

Face heating, I force out a weak smile, then race to the restrooms, running through a list in my head of what I need to do. Wash my hands first and foremost, fix my hair, take some deep breaths—"Oh!" I collide with someone coming around the corner. My hand lifts during the impact, which means—the brown gunk on my hand is now on whoever I just ran into.

"Oh no."

Alex. It had to be Alex.

Strong hands grip my arms in a steadying hold. "Jane. Oh. What is this?" He's eyeing the brown spot on his worn-out Led Zeppelin T-shirt with a mixture of confusion and revulsion.

"BART incident."

His bright green eyes meet mine, filling with amusement, and then he smiles. The world spins to a stop and my heart flip-flops in my chest.

Alex is my not-so-secret crush, a fact that has me turning bright red every time he comes within a sixty-foot radius.

And now, he's touching me.

"Ah. You were on your way to mitigate the situation." He releases me, shoving his hands in the pockets of his jeans and inclining his head in the direction of the bathrooms.

"Think of yourself as collateral damage." I smile and heat floods my face. I managed to say something without sounding like a total dork, so of course I'm going to turn bright red.

Despite the fact that Alex and I have worked closely together for months, I still can't keep my shit together around him. And it's worse now, after what happened in the storage closet right behind him.

Don't think about it, Jane. Don't remember or you'll make it worse.

It's not apparent at first glance, but Alex is kind of a big deal. He started developing gaming apps as a teenager and made his first million just this past year.

About six months ago, he hired Blue Wave to help him market his newest releases. I was on his team initially, but then, of course, I screwed it up and was transferred off his team two months ago. Since then, I only see him when he stops by the office for meetings or to drop things off or whatever business he has now.

It's for the best, really. If I don't see him every day, then I can't waste my time imagining running my hands through his shaggy hair, which is eternally a week away from needing a haircut. I also can't think about what it would be like to bite that spot at the side of his jaw, just under his ear, or what his perfectly symmetrical lips would feel like against mine.

Nope. Can't spend time on any of that, because it's like wishing on a star, or buying a lotto ticket, or forwarding a chain email to obtain true happiness. Nice in theory, but impossible in reality.

"I get it, I'm damaged goods," he says with a grin.

I chuckle and try to rein in my galloping heart rate. "Yeah, you're a hot mess." I wave a hand. "I-I'm kidding. I'm just giving you a hard-on." The world freezes to a halt.

Our eyes lock.

His brows lift.

I replay the words in my head. *Nope.* "Hard *time!*"

And now I'm yelling at him. "Hard *time*. *Not* hard-on."
The heat in my face is an inferno. A volcano. My head
might erupt.

Alex is laughing his ass off while I die inside slowly.
I try to force out a laugh. I can laugh at myself, it's why
I'm still somewhat functional, but really, I would
rather cry.

Why is it so hard for me to talk to him without
making a fool of myself?

"Oh, Jane." He wipes his eyes. "I miss talking to
you."

My heart leaps in my chest before making a crash
landing. *He's* the one who asked for me to be removed
from his team.

I liked Alex in a more than professional way, and
I'm sure that's why I was taken off of his team. He
would never say so, of course. He's too nice to tell me to
my face how much I embarrassed myself.

My face burns even hotter.

It doesn't matter. I have a boyfriend now. Mark.
Even though we've never gone on an actual date, we're
sort of together—I mean, we've been sleeping together
for the past two months, so we're something. Definitely
something. Even though I'm not sure I like Mark.

Ugh.

I kick thoughts of Mark away.

Alex smiles at me when the laughter dies down. "I
won't keep you. You have a pitch or something today,
right? For the senior marketing job?"

"Oh, yes. And unfortunately, I'm late."

"I'm sure you'll do great."

"Thanks, Alex. You're a good friend."

And that's all he'll ever be. Guys like him don't go for women like me. Especially after I smeared what may or may not be excrement all over him.

His smile slips a little, or I imagine it does, because it's just a second and then it's as bright as ever. "Good luck." He has dimples.

Ugh, so cute.

Washing up in the bathroom, I glance in the mirror and groan. I look like I went through a typhoon to get here. I can't believe Alex saw me like this. I attempt to straighten my crazy hair and clean the mascara off my cheek.

And then I take one final, deep breath before picking up my briefcase and heading out the door.

Chapter Two

THE LIMBIC SYSTEM IS AN EXTRAORDINARY PART OF THE human brain, especially when it comes to survival. It regulates heart rate, body temperature, and a myriad of other basic functions. But it also constantly scans the environment for possible threats. It's important if you're, say, walking through a jungle and you come across a hungry tiger crouching in the bushes waiting for its next meal. It gives you adrenaline, strength, and speed, and it helps you fight the threat or flee the danger.

But if I'm going to talk in front of a group of people, or interact with people at all, my limbic system becomes an inconvenient burden.

Not only does my brain scan the environment for crouching tigers, it scans the social environment for cues of danger, real or imagined. And past experience has informed my brain time and time again that danger is everywhere, always, and it's impossible to tell my limbic system otherwise.

This is why, as I pass through the employee area and make my way to the other side of the building, my heart races, my hands shake, and my throat closes up. The stark white hallway to the conference room is empty, but apparently my brain thinks it's a life-or-death situation.

I stand there, staring at the shut door and trying to regain control of my body. They're in there.

One more calming breath, which does nothing to slow my racing heart, and then I'm in.

"Hello. Sorry I'm late." My voice only shakes a little.

"That's fine, Jane. Please, have a seat." Stacey offers me a smile that I think is supposed to be comforting, but my heart is still pounding and a trickle of sweat slips down my side.

I really hope I don't get pit stains in the middle of all this.

Mother's voice whispers in my head. *Be strong. Don't screw this up. Stewarts never give up and we never fail.* The same things she would say every time I had to do anything important, from a school performance to taking the SATs to applying for college. Like any failure of mine, big or small, would somehow tarnish her success.

The team leaders are waiting for me in a circle of white pillows on the floor. Not bed pillows, but specially designed seating pillows. A custom-made glass table sits in front of them, low to the ground.

"We're ready when you are," Blade says. Blade has dark hair and beady eyes and is about twenty-five, my age. I'm pretty sure his real name is John.

I shuffle over to the pillow situated across from them and set my briefcase on the floor, plopping myself down too quickly, which causes my pants to hit the taut fabric of the pillow at just the right angle to make . . . a fart sound. That's the only way to describe it.

The ensuing silence is an oppressive presence in the room, smothering me in a vise-like grip.

My hot face gets hotter. I clear my throat.

Stacey smiles encouragingly. She's the nicest one on the team, in her late thirties, with short brown hair and black rimmed glasses.

Sitting on Blade's right, Drew is completely stone-faced. He's bald and never smiles and I'm pretty sure he's actually a cyborg.

Finally, Blade motions with a hand. "Being the focus of attention is something you'll have to get used to for the position you want. It's best to get started."

"Right." I pull the papers from my case with shaky fingers.

It's a pitch for a twenty-second video ad for a life-style app. The app combines social media with restaurant recommendations and food reviews. It notifies you if a friend is eating within a certain radius by sending an alert. You can also read friends' notes and reviews on various establishments. I've never really understood the need to brag about what you're eating. And alerting people to where you are? Doesn't appeal to me in the slightest. What if you don't want to be found? I guess that doesn't matter. What matters is this is my job, and a new client has spent a boatload to have the video air in the middle of other videos for some up-and-coming YouTubers who have bajillions of viewers. So basically, we can't screw this up.

"Here are details and a cost analysis. And my idea for the, uh, video." I clear my throat again and shuffle my paperwork.

They take the pages from my trembling fingers. I breathe in slow and deep, trying to calm my heart rate. I've practiced this pitch a thousand times. I can do this.

"It, um, it opens with a restaurant at night." My voice is pitched too high and too loud. I stop, clear my throat and try to speak at a normal volume. "There's a, uh, glowing ambiance, you know, soft lighting, it's very warm and aesthetically pleasing. The camera follows a waiter moving around the restaurant, bringing people plates. Eventually he stops on a large group of friends. They're laughing, enjoying the meal, barely noticing he's there. And then the ad line comes up on the screen, I'm thinking a happy, bouncy, font that's also readable, and it says, 'Enjoy more of life with Splice.' "

Stacey puts down her paper and gives me an encouraging smile to continue. The others are silent. Drew is frowning down at the paperwork and Blade seems to be staring somewhere off to the side but slightly down, like he's pretending to look at it.

"It's short, but effective. The concept cuts down the ad time, which will save the client money, while still getting the point across as to the purpose of the app, and it's more likely to keep viewers engaged."

Drew and Blade share a glance and then Drew speaks. "It's fine, Jane, but it's not quite there."

My tongue sticks to the roof of my mouth.

"It lacks emotion. In fact, a lot of the ideas you've proposed in the past have this same flaw. I know you've been given this feedback before. The best ads give some kind of emotional impact, or nostalgia, something that makes people relate and feel."

"I lack emotion?" My voice rises. This can't be true. Emotion is making my entire body hot and cold. It's why there are invisible ants crawling all over my skin. My mind is frozen, trying to take in what he's saying but not quite absorbing the words. If this isn't emotion, what is?

Stacey winces. "It's not that you lack emotion, personally. It's that your ads lack emotion."

Blade shuffles the papers in his hands, not meeting my eyes. "And you don't have enough experience and it shows."

I swallow past the lump in my throat. "I've worked here for four years," I mumble. I'm here all the time. I always stay late. I've never even taken a sick day.

Meanwhile half the office calls in on Mondays to nurse their hangovers. But I complete all their grunt work, filing, and reports, without complaint. And this is what I get in return?

Stacey says, "You're a hard worker, Jane, but you aren't good at explaining your ideas. They don't come across in a clear manner. This job doesn't come as easily to you as some of your peers and that's not necessarily your fault."

Drew sighs. "What we're saying here, Jane, is that even with the extra time on the job, you're not producing as much usable content. Not enough to run your own team, barely enough to make it as a student marketer."

Prickly heat coats my skin. "I'll work harder."

"It's not that, it's just . . . you don't fit," Blade says.

And there it is. Something I've heard over and over. You'd think it would be less of a shock after a while, but it's not. I don't fit in anywhere. Not here, not with any type of friends group, not at work, not even with my family.

Drew taps his pen against the glass table. "The truth is, Jane, this pitch was one last shot to see if you had anything to offer this company. And you don't."

"Is this—are you . . . firing me?"

"Yes." Blade is abrupt.

Stacey shoots him a dirty look and leans toward me. "You shouldn't think of this as a door shutting. It's a whole bunch of new doors ready to open. You need to find your niche. And this isn't it, Jane. You're too shy."

Her words don't quite register through the roar of blood in my ears.

Fired.

I'm being fired.

Everything dims, blackness infiltrating the edges of my vision. The walls of the room press in on me.

In a daze, I shut my briefcase and snap it closed. Then I grab up the papers scattered all over the table, pressing them to my chest since I don't want to take the time to stop and open my briefcase again. Pages crumple in my hands as I heave myself to my feet.

Somehow, I make it out of the room, the door swinging closed behind me with an unsatisfying whisper of a click.

I don't say anything. Not goodbye. Not so long. Not you're welcome for the hard work, assholes.

Standing in the all-white hallway, I focus on my breathing. I crouch on the ground and open my briefcase, shoving the papers inside with numb hands before standing again.

I need to get out of here before I have a full-blown panic attack.

My gaze lifts, down the hall, toward the bullpen, where the other employees are working.

I can't face them. What if everyone knows? What if they've all talked about this? What if they all voted and unanimously decided to kick the antisocial loser off the island?

Hannah will be happy.

I have to pack up my desk, but I need a minute to pull myself together.

Moving fast, I walk past the main sitting area with my head down, not making eye contact, and let out a sigh of relief when I reach the corridor to the bathroom.

But before I make it to a place where I can lose my shit in peace, Mark is there.

"Hey, Jane. Come with me." He grabs my hand, tugging me to the door opposite the bathroom. The storage room. Somewhere we've fooled around before.

Once inside the tiny space crammed with supplies and glowing with the faint red light from an old printer, he shuts the door. Then his mouth presses hard against mine. He fumbles with the hem of my blouse, yanking it out of my pants to run insistent fingers over my stomach.

I'm not in the mood, a maelstrom of shock and nerves and everything else running through the stomach he's currently caressing, but I don't make any move to stop him. Besides, maybe this will help me relax, to think about something other than the fact that the job I've been working toward for the last four years ended in the space of a heartbeat.

He tugs my pants down and lifts me against the wall. I try to lose myself in the act. He's a good kisser. He's attractive. Blond hair, blue eyes, straight teeth. I'm lucky he shows any interest in me at all.

Plain Jane. Shy Jane. Jane who just got fired.

I shove the thoughts away, trying to focus on the physical sensations instead of the emotions roiling through me, but it doesn't quite last long enough for me to enjoy anything.

He groans and shudders and exhales a hot breath against my neck.

Well. I'm glad he's feeling better.

Something sharp jabs me in the side, a nail or some-thing sticking out of the wall at my back. Great. Now there's a tear in my shirt.

He drops my legs and turns away.

I grab my slacks from the floor, sliding them back on.

It's always like this with Mark, quick, brutal, and fevered.

At first, it all seemed so romantic. Like he's starved and desperate for me. Like he wants me. He needs me. *Me.* I'm important. A heady feeling for someone who's never been in demand for anything or anyone.

But in this moment, insight wedges open a crack in my mind, bringing a light so piercing that what it illumi-nates has to be true: a thought I've been missing, or more likely, avoiding. This isn't a rush of lust, must-have-you-or-die kind of frenzy. It's a more frantic and panicked and I-have-to-escape-this-right-now kind of frenzy.

"How was that for a stress reliever?" He tosses me a smirk over his shoulder, disposing of the condom in a trash can in the corner.

It was about as stress relieving as a root canal. "Great. Except my pitch didn't go so great. They . . ." I swallow. I can't even say it.

But he speaks before I can shove the rest of the words out, pulling up his skinny distressed jeans and turning to face me. "I'm sure it'll be fine. Hey, Presley's your friend. You think she'll go out with me?"

I blink. "What?"

"Presley."

Blood rushes from my head to my toes, making me lightheaded. This cannot be happening. Is he really asking me about another woman after we . . . after we just—?

"You two are friends, right? You're like the only one she really talks to."

"Um—"

He steps closer, crowding me against the wall in the cramped space. "I know she's only worked here for a few months, but she seems to like you, so I just thought you might have some inside intel."

I'm frozen. My mouth is full of cotton. *Say something.* "Oh. Yeah. I mean, Presley is great. I, um, I, uh, didn't know we were seeing other people."

"Who? Me and you?" His brows lift in surprise.

"I-I thought we were like, casually dating or something?" It's not an irrational assumption, is it? Considering he was just inside me?

He chuckles and rubs my arms. It's not a soothing motion. It makes my skin crawl.

What am I doing? Have I really spent the last two months sleeping with him just because I have no other options?

"Casual being the operative word there, sweetheart."

His smile is light, bemused. Like I'm a cute little bunny who's being silly.

When I don't smile back, his lips droop. "Wait. You aren't upset, right? We never said we were exclusive or anything. I mean, hell, Jane, we haven't even hung out outside work."

"No. No. You-you're right. It's-it's fine." The stammer gives me away. It always does.

And it's not fine. My cheeks burn. Shame squirms under my skin. Why did I fall for his flirting and compliments and secret grins? I'm an idiot.

"Good. I want us to be friends and I was thinking about asking Presley out. You'd be cool with that, right?"

Swallowing past my tongue, which has suddenly swollen in my mouth, I manage to eke out an answer. "Yeah. That's fine. Totally . . . fine. I have to—"

I have to get out of here.

I flee the room like it's on fire, stalking across the hall to the bathroom, my vision crowding with black spots. Once in a stall, I sit and breathe. I have to force the air in and out slowly, counting, counting, counting until my heart evens out.

It's not like I'm in love with Mark or anything, I just thought . . . My jaw clenches. I saw what I wanted to see. I was so eager for someone to *see* me that I would have taken anyone that showed the slightest bit of interest.

Bright side. There has to be a bright side.

I'm still alive. I paid my rent for this month, so I have a few weeks until I have to worry about being homeless. And I guess I won't have to worry about things being strained around Mark since I no longer have a job here.

A wet giggle bursts out of me, an abrupt and braying noise, echoing in the tiled bathroom.

A toilet flushes.

Aaand, of course, I'm not alone in here.

Why me?

A few minutes later, I'm standing at my desk, eyes tracing over the contents scattered across the surface: sticky notes, highlighters, the pens lined up neatly next to where I normally set my laptop.

I guess I came over to pack up my desk, but why? Nothing here is mine. I have no photos, no plants, no personal items. It all belongs to them.

"How did it go?" Presley stops at the corner of my desk.

"Fine." An automatic response to everything in my life. It's all fine. Even when it's decidedly not fine. Just smile and keep going. That's what I do.

"You don't look fine."

My head doesn't quite shake. It tilts. "Yeah. I'm not."

"Oh no. Do you want to talk about it? We could take an early lunch."

Early lunch? I don't have a lunch hour, not anymore. All day will be my lunch. I swallow down some strangled, hysterical laugh threatening to emerge like a drunk hyena.

"No. I've got to go." I lift my gaze.

She's always been kind to me. She's never made snide comments when I stumble over my words or spout random things irrelevant to the current topic when my mind bounces away from me, and she's offered to go to lunch at least once a week since she started.

And now Mark wants to add her to his list of office hookups. And I can't hate her. I'm not sure I actually care if Mark wants her, but I worry a little for her sake.

"Thank you, Presley. For everything."

She shrugs. "No problem. I'll see you tomorrow?"

"Sure." There's no point in telling her I'm not coming back. It's not like anyone here, even Presley, would notice or care for more than a blip before moving on with their lives.

Chapter Three

OUTSIDE, IT'S A DREARY AND GRIM FOGGY MORNING IN San Francisco.

Karl. That's what locals call the incessant fog that rolls in, especially prevalent in the June months. Karl even has his own Instagram account. I squint up into the gray haze.

It's perfect.

I'm halfway down the block, fingering the tear in the side of my nicest blouse, wondering how I'm going to explain to my parents that I got *fired*, when footsteps slap the pavement behind me.

"Hey, Jane. You okay?"

I stop and turn around in the middle of the sidewalk, letting Alex catch up to me.

This is a horrible time to have to talk like a normal person to my biggest male fantasy brought to life. This day is like every awful thing I thought would ever happen to me coming true. I always tried to tell myself it was the anxiety talking, but this time the anxiety was right.

I'm doomed.

"My shirt ripped," I tell him. I've reverted to a toddler who's got an owie and can only focus on one thing.

He regards me, head tilted, eyes concerned.

Now I'll have to wear the blue shirt to job interviews, but it's a little on the tight side and the button right in front of my boobs always pops open. I guess that's one way to get a job. If I can even get another job. I guess I could apply to other marketing firms but it will mean starting all over again. How to explain my sudden departure from Blue Wave? I doubt they'll give me a nice reference. On top of that, I'm terrible at interviews. I was lucky to get my job at Blue Wave.

Lucky. Ha.

"I might have a safety pin in the truck." He shoves his hands in his pockets. "Just wait here a sec?"

I nod. I have nowhere else to be.

The air is heavy with moisture. I forgot to grab a jacket. My hand clenches on the handle of my briefcase. Random people pass me on the sidewalk. A couple holding hands. A man jogging. A group of teenagers laughing. Are they laughing at me? Probably. I'm standing on the sidewalk alone, out of it, clothing ripped. I can't even imagine what I might look like right now.

Alex comes jogging back, holding up a safety pin. "Here."

I take it, our fingers brushing, eyes locking for a heated split second.

Alex wouldn't be greedy in bed, like Mark. He would never use anyone for an escape. Oh no. I bet when Alex takes a woman to bed, he takes his time and makes sure everyone is satisfied.

Not that I'll ever know.

The acidic taste of regret rises in my throat.

Setting my briefcase on the ground, I twist to work on my shirt.

"So, how did the meeting go?" he asks.

I pinch the fabric together with one hand and slip the safety pin in. "Not great."

"Oh no. I was going to tease you about the hard-on comment, but now I'd feel like a dick."

He smiles, waiting for me to respond to the joke, but it's not in me.

"Are you all right? Are you not feeling well, is that why you're leaving? You seem a little . . . distracted." He glances back at the building behind us. "You never take a day off."

"I'm fine. I—"

I want to tell him. The words are poised at the tip of my tongue, ready to dive into the open. I want comfort. I want reassurance it will all be okay.

But I can't tell him. I'm itchy with embarrassment. Everything is all wrong.

I want to run away and run into his arms all at the same time. I need to get out of here.

Finished with the safety pin, I pick up my briefcase. "I've got to go."

"Do you need a ride somewhere?"

"No. I'm fine. Thanks though. Bye, Alex."

Goodbye forever, an overly dramatic voice in my head intones.

Wild laughter threatens to erupt out of my mouth, but I choke it down and keep walking. Maybe I should be crying. I mean, everything I've been working for is over in a blink, but it's like it's too overwhelming to process.

I don't know where to go. Back to my empty apartment? I don't think so. I pass by the Embarcadero train station and keep walking.

I barely remember crossing Broadway, but I end up in North Beach down by the piers, a wide stretch of sidewalk punctuated every hundred feet or so by wooden docks and a variety of stores and restaurants.

I don't know what to do with myself. I have no one to talk to.

Even if I did, my phone is broken.

My phone.

I breathe in the sea- and fish-laced air and sit down on a bench facing the fog-drenched bay. Pulling my phone from my briefcase, I squint at the dead screen. I take it apart, messing with the battery, putting it back together. Nothing works.

I give up. What does it matter? Who am I going to call? My parents? Ha!

They are the last people I want to explain my most recent failure to. I slump down on the bench, rubbing my head.

I don't know how long I sit there, surrounded by thick mist, tourists, and locals running along the piers. I sit there until the chilly wind from the bay seeps in, my hands go numb, and my feet are freezing in my sensible low heels.

Eventually I pick myself up and trudge back to the train that will take me across the bay into Emeryville.

Walking home, I stop in the shopping center near my apartment for Thai takeout and a bottle of wine. Might as well spend money I don't have on comfort food and booze.

It's dark by the time I get home. Thankfully, I don't run into anyone in my building. And there's no rap thumping through the walls, so that's something.

I open my door and step on a small square of paper that someone must have shoved under the door.

I set my briefcase and the bag of food on the counter.

YOU MUST BE AT WORK. I tried to call but your phone keeps going to voicemail. Call me?
  -Eloise

. . .

MY SISTER. My sister the actress, who's already had a successful series on Netflix even though she's two years younger than me, and she has some fancy director boyfriend she met on set and they're both in love and beautiful. Oh, *and* she's taking a break from acting because she got accepted to Stanford.

So glad I didn't come home early and run into her on accident.

I crumple up her note and throw it in the trash.

Grabbing a fork, I open the takeout container and shovel in a forkful of yellow curry, but my stomach revolts.

I can't eat yet. I put the food in the fridge and then stare at the wine bottle for a second. The top is a screw off.

Going into the living room, I sit on the edge of the couch. Twisting the cap off the wine, I take a swig directly from the bottle. Then another. And another.

Deep breath. I screw the lid back on and hold it against my chest before flopping backward onto the couch.

I gaze up at my ceiling.

The couch is old and used and a spring digs into my butt. But it's all I could afford.

I sit up to drink more before plopping back again.

Wallowing in despair is inevitable. But my last therapist always told me when it seems like everything is falling apart, focus on the things you can be grateful for. Because there's always something, no matter how small it might seem.

I drink more and glance around my apartment. I love it here. It's small and basic. One bedroom, one bathroom, tiny kitchen and living space, but it's mine. It's not like I need anything fancy. I'm not a scientist like my parents—I take another drink on that thought—and I'm not a brilliant hottie like Eloise—I take two drinks on that one. I just need a job good enough to pay for this apartment. This lovely apartment I love. The best part is the tub, one of those old-fashioned claw-foot things.

More wine goes down my throat. I feel so much better now.

I love this wine.

I love my tub. I love my apartment.

Love is a weird word. Love love love.

I love Alex. Nope.

Where did that thought come from? I don't love Alex, he's too good for me.

Someone is crying. Is it me? I pat my cheeks. No. Not me. Another swig of wine down the gullet. I'm not having a meltdown and it's all thanks to this lovely wine.

My body is warm. Too warm. I go from warm and fuzzy to hot and uncomfortable in quick succession. Time to go enjoy my tub while I can still afford soap.

I stumble into the bathroom, setting my wine on the counter, and then tug off my clothes. I hate these clothes. I shove them in the tiny bathroom trash and then get into the empty tub in my bra and undies.

A quiet sob fills the space.

Is that me? No, I pat my chest, no sobbing coming from in here. I'm not crying but someone is.

My eyes drift shut. I'm dizzy. Tired. So tired. Who is crying?

Ugh. I'm not the only one who had a terrible Monday. I'm so glad this day is over.

Chapter Four

BUUUUUURP.

Groaning I roll over, tugging my pillow over my head.

What the heck?

It's the same song. Spackle me? Is that what he's saying?

Sleep recedes, reality intrudes. Brain fires up, trying to make sense of the noise.

Does the neighbor play this every morning? I guess I wouldn't know, since I'm usually gone by now. But today . . . I have nowhere to be today, because I am ungainfully unemployed. I guess I should get up and look for a job at least. But I don't want to do anything except hide forever.

I'm probably hungover.

I take a second to assess my physical well-being, bracing myself for pain, but . . . I'm fine. My brain is clear, if still slightly groggy from sleep. No aches or pains. My head should be killing me with the racket thumping through the walls. But there's nothing. No dry mouth, no nausea, no anything.

I'm not hungover at all, which shouldn't be the case since I don't drink much and the amount I ingested yesterday was enough to inebriate at least three of me.

Wait, didn't I fall asleep in the bathtub last night? I must have been really out of it because I don't even remember climbing into bed.

Knock knock knock.

Someone's at the door. What time is it?

Stumbling out of bed, I glance down. I'm in my ducky PJs. Didn't I throw these in the hamper yesterday?

More knocking. Maybe it's Eloise stalking me since my phone is still dead.

My phone. Which is on my bedside table. I pick it up and stare at the blank screen. Didn't I mess with it yesterday and throw it in my briefcase?

I didn't touch my briefcase once I started drinking, so it should still be in the . . . nope. I come to an abrupt halt next to my desk. The briefcase is here. On the floor, perpendicular to the wall. This is where I normally put it, but last night, I dumped it in the kitchen. I know it.

Knocking again.

"Coming! I'm coming."

I open the door.

The neighbor in the red robe. He's knocking on Hugo's door again.

"Hugo! Come on, man, it can't be that bad."

I blink at him. Is this like, a daily routine they have?

He pounds on the door again. "It's Monday! I have a meeting in thirty minutes, Hugo. Help me out here, huh?"

"Monday?" The word whispers out of my mouth, inaudible under the music.

No. That's not right. What is this, some kind of performance art or something?

I stare at my neighbor until he turns away from Hugo's door and catches me.

"Hey." He nods and shuffles over to his door, across the hall from mine.

"I'm sorry, did you say Monday?" I yell over the din.

"What?" A crease forms between his bushy salt-and-pepper brows.

"Today is Tuesday," I tell him.

He frowns. "No. It's Monday."

"It can't be Monday. Yesterday was Monday."

He rolls his eyes and pulls his own phone out of a deep pocket in his robe. "Here." He holds it up, facing me.

"It's the—" I blink at the impossible date. "It is the seventh." I'm frozen, staring at the digital *June 7th* like it might morph itself to *8th* right before my very eyes.

When he pulls the phone away, I grab his arm to keep it in my sight. "It's the seventh." It's really the seventh. "Oh my gosh I had the worst dream last night." I release him to press a hand to my head.

I can't process this.

"Oh crap, I'm late. Again!" I spin around and slam the door behind me.

Dizzy with adrenaline and nerves and confusion, I get dressed and grab my makeup bag. Déjà vu rushes through me. This is so bizarre. The outfit I laid out is there, on the chair in my bedroom. There's no tear in the side of my blouse, no gold safety pin from Alex. I smooth it out, staring hard at the side that was ripped. Yesterday. Or so I thought. Was it really a dream? I've never had such a vivid dream. Or nightmare, more like. But it didn't really happen. It couldn't have.

Relief blows through me like a spring breeze. I won't get fired. Things will be back to normal. I'll do fine on my pitch. I won't get fired. It will be great.

But the fuzzy, warm feelings are short-lived.

On the train, it's just like my dream. Redhead with bright clothes. Business dude flailing his hands and talking.

The train lurches and I reach for the pole again.

I lift my hand into my field of vision. Again with the brown questionable substance.

I stare at it, my mind going a mile a minute, my heart picking up in time with my racing thoughts. What if I'm psychic now? Is this what it's like for psychic people? One day you know everything that's going to happen?

I should be rushing to work, but the sense of discombobulation won't leave and it makes me feel like I'm walking through water.

"Hannah, can you—?" The words stall out in my mouth.

Her nose twitches like she's smelling something rank. Exactly like in my dream.

"Hey, Jane." Presley appears behind her, a brow puckered. "You look like you need a sec. I'll tell the team you're here and will be with them in a minute."

I can't even say thanks this time. I nod and turn in the direction of the bathrooms.

But not before I catch Mark's sly wink, making me flinch.

I approach the hallway to the bathroom like a heroine in a horror flick approaching the basement with a broken light.

I want to wash my dirty hand more than I want to breathe, but . . . if Alex . . .

"Hey, Jane." He emerges from the hallway leading to the restrooms and stops in front of me.

I exhale a relieved breath. And then I stare. He's wearing the same shirt. The Led Zeppelin tee I got dirty yesterday.

I look down at my hand. Well, at least this is different. Not everything matches my nightmare Monday.

"Your interview is today, right?" he asks.

I lift my gaze to his. "Have you ever had déjà vu?"

His brows lift. "Yeah, sure." Head tilts. "Are you okay?"

Am I okay? "I had a terrible nightmare and it's like . . . it didn't end."

A wrinkle forms between his brows. "Is there anything I can—"

What am I doing, telling Alex about my problems? Like he needs a reminder about how pathetic I am. "It's nothing. I gotta go. I'm late."

I step around him and make it to the bathroom, once again engaging in a futile attempt to fix my hair and makeup. I take a few deep breaths. I can do this. But can I? Can I handle being fired again? What if it doesn't happen the same? Maybe it will be different. It has to be different. With Alex, it was different.

Then it's back down the pristine hallway of doom.

I open the conference room door, holding my breath.

Stacey, Blade, and Drew are all there. Dressed the same, sitting the same on those damn pillows.

"Good morning. Sorry I'm late."

"That's fine, Jane. Please, have a seat," Stacey says.

I don't sit. There's no way I'm repeating the fart noise from yesterday. I hand out the materials and loom over them like some kind of awkward overlord.

This is the worst.

Don't panic, Jane. Breathe.

But my newfound psychic ability doesn't cease the inevitable conclusion.

I give my pitch. The same, practiced pitch.

And it's the same exact shit show where everything they said in my dream is repeated nearly verbatim.

I don't fit in.

Okay, universe, got the message during middle school but feel free to keep it coming.

I leave the conference room just as I did yesterday, but the shock and dismay and depression—which are all still there but not as prevalent—are being shoved aside in favor of confusion and panic.

I have to get out of here. I need space to think.

Even my thoughts are the same.

Then Mark is there, grabbing my hand. I follow him on autopilot. Again I'm tugged into the closet. Even knowing the conclusion of this particular story line, I don't say no. I don't put up a fight. I let it happen.

I should tell him no. After all, he's using me. I've known, probably the whole time, and just didn't want to believe it. I shouldn't do this. Logically, I know it, but the truth is I crave the contact, such as it is. I'm using him as much as he's using me. It doesn't make it right. It doesn't make sense.

And I still do it.

My shirt rips. I didn't even feel the nail poking me this time.

What is wrong with me? What is wrong with today?

Mark is talking. I don't have to listen to know what he's saying.

It's the same one-sided conversation, made even more so because I don't think I could speak up if I tried.

"I know she's only worked here for a few months,

but she seems to like you, so I just thought you might have some inside intel."

Without a word in response, I straighten my clothes and leave him in the closet.

And then, I'm back at my desk, staring at the gray stapler set precisely in the corner.

"Hey, are you okay?" Presley.

I meet her worried gaze. "I'm not sure."

"How did it go?"

I stare at her for a few long seconds and then step to the side, toward the exit.

"Wait, do you want to talk about it? We could take an early lunch."

My head shakes slowly. "Maybe tomorrow." My gaze tips down to the hole in my nicest shirt. "I should have been prepared for this," I mutter.

"Prepared for what?"

My head snaps up. "Nothing."

Outside, as I walk briskly away from the office, it happens again. Footsteps behind me.

I turn around before he speaks.

Alex stops a few feet away, concern scrawled across his face. "Hey, Jane. You okay?"

"I . . . I'm fine." I'm not fine. I cross my arms over my chest to hide the tear in my shirt. I need to get out of here. Run. Hide. My shock is wearing off and my brain is screaming danger, *danger*.

"How did it go?"

"Um. It was fine. Just fine."

"Are you all right? Are you not feeling well, is that

why you're leaving?" He glances back at the building behind us. "You never take time off."

"It's nothing I . . . yes, I might be coming down with something." I look away from his concerned gaze. It's almost too much to take after what I just did with Mark in the closet. Again!

I don't deserve sympathy. I deserve everything this horrible day has thrown at me. Twice.

"Do you need a ride?"

"No. No thanks. Bye, Alex."

There's no wandering the piers for me today. I take the next available train home.

This time, I'm not drinking.

Instead, I stress clean, scrubbing my frustrations out on my bathtub, the grout in the kitchen tiles, even the baseboards while my mind tries to make sense of everything that happened today. Yesterday. Whatever. When I'm done, I'm hot and sweaty and starving, and I still have no idea what the heck is going on with my life. I order delivery from the Elephant Bar down the street, too scared to leave my apartment again. It's a jungle out there.

When the food arrives, I pay the delivery guy and step on a piece of paper that's been shoved under the door.

Eloise.

It's the same note as before, except I was home all day and didn't hear her knocking. Maybe I missed it over all the excessive cleansing.

I take the food and my laptop into the living room. I

want to google stuff about mental health and dreaming things that then come true. But after pushing on the power button multiple times, followed by every other button on the keyboard, it doesn't turn on. Dead. Why are all my electronics on the fritz?

I put the ripped blouse in the closet on top of my old sewing supplies, pausing for just a second to touch a bit of satin and chiffon I bought years ago at a craft store in the city. A purchase from back when I first moved here and had design dreams dancing in my head. Dreams that were crushed inch by inch with every day spent at Blue Wave, every time I put on a black or gray sensible outfit, every phone call from Mother exhorting me to work harder, to be better, until there was nothing left.

With purposeful movements, I place my cell phone inside a paper bag and then put in in my briefcase, closing up the whole thing and setting it in the bath-room, under the sink, then closing the bathroom door to keep everything inside. I triple and quadruple check my ducky PJs are in the hamper. Then I put on an old oversize *Les Mis* T-shirt.

I get in bed and stare at the ceiling.

I can't sleep, the thoughts spinning and lurching through my mind like a busted merry-go-round.

When Mark first started flirting with me, I ignored him. Avoided him. I thought he was messing with me, and I'm good at avoidance, it's practically an art. But he was persistent.

After the first month of constant attention, compliments, and flirting, I started to believe he actually liked me.

He told me he appreciated my shyness and nerves. It made me different. Unique. He thought it was cute.

Then we were at the office late one night working on a project alone. He kissed me, and then we . . . well, it went further. And then it turned into a thing. But only around the office. Over the course of a month or two, the thoughtfulness and conversation became less and less until it was purely physical.

I should have stopped it before. I was weak. I am weak, and I regret it. All of it.

This whole day is an exposure of every fault I've tried to hide, every time I've tried to pretend I'm happy when I'm not.

I lie in the dark forever, judging myself and coming up lacking over and over.

I can't sleep.

Then the broken sobs whisper through the walls.

This happened last night too. Or this night. Whatever. I thought it was me drunk weeping, but it's not.

It's coming from Hugo's. The music man. Why is he sad? His cries are the perfect soundtrack to the past two days. One day. Ugh.

I take deep breaths and try to calm my mind. I just need some sleep.

Tomorrow will be better. Tomorrow will be Tuesday. This was just a weird blip. It has to be.

Otherwise . . . what if I'm dead? Or something is

wrong with me? Anxious thoughts crowd my head. I can't let myself spiral.

I focus on my breathing.

Everything will work out. It always does . . . doesn't it?

Chapter Five

BURPING.

Music bumping.

Bass thumping.

I open my eyes and stare up at my ceiling, moving from dead sleep to full-blown panic in half a second.

What is *happening*?

I lurch up in bed, taking in the contents of my bedroom with a sharp glance.

My briefcase is there, next to my desk.

"No. No no no no no."

I'm in the ducky PJs. My phone's on the nightstand. I pick it up. Dead.

I try to take deep breaths, but I can't. My throat closes up. It's not working. I think I might throw up. Black spots cloud my vision.

"Sprinkle me," the music says.

"Sprinkle yourself!" I yell and then immediately gasp for air.

Blackness surrounds me, coalescing into a dark tunnel of denial, anger, shock, depression, you name it. I'm a living stew of swirling emotions.

Knocking.

I'm breathing heavy, air sawing in and out, and still I go out to the hall and stare at neighbor man in his red robe outside Hugo's door.

"It's Monday! I have a call in thirty minutes. Help me out here, huh?"

I slam the door, leaning back against it and blindly staring into the living room. I haven't had a full-blown panic attack in a while. I've been safe. I've had a routine. I've avoided doing things that trigger too much anxiety. And now, all of that hard work has been shattered to smithereens.

Think, Jane, think.

I race into my bedroom. I can't make sense of any of this. What do I do? Isn't the definition of insanity doing the same thing over and over and expecting something to change?

But what are my other options? Hiding from the world sounds great, but . . .

I stop by the chair in my bedroom and stare at the clothes set out. The blouse is gone. Only the pants are there, laying in the same position they were the past two days. The shirt's missing. Why is the shirt missing?

I open the closet. There it is. Where I put it, yesterday, which was also Monday. The blouse is still there, on the sewing box. I pick it up. And it's still ripped.

My mind isn't working at an efficient enough pace to figure this puzzle out. It's still Monday. Yesterday, the second Monday, when I woke up, the tear was gone and it was sitting on the chair, where I had left it before. What does this mean? Why is this the only thing that's different? *Is* this the only thing that's different?

I press both hands against my head. Why did the torn shirt stay in the closet where I put it, but everything else is the same as it was that first Monday? But it's still Monday!

The closet is magic? Sounds about as rational as any other theory right now.

There's no time to ponder the ramifications of a mystical closet. I have to go to work. I have to . . . Why am I going back there to be fired again? How can I make it different? How can I prevent being fired? What if I can keep my job somehow? What if this whole thing is an opportunity to get it right?

I stare at my briefcase. Maybe I shouldn't go to work. But what if today is different? The shirt thing was already different. I can't risk it. What if today I don't get fired? What if Mark doesn't . . . ugh I don't want to be with Mark, even if he suddenly decides he loves me and wants to run away together and get married and have a million babies. My stomach wrenches at the thought of yesterday. Both yesterdays.

I can't do that to myself. Not anymore. But the thought of confronting him makes me equally sick. I don't even want to talk to him. What do I do? Maybe I can find a way to avoid him. Good ol' reliable plan B.

I make it out of the apartment building to the sidewalk, wearing the blue boobie blouse. My gaze drops periodically to check out the buttonhole situation, which is precarious at best.

One thing I can do . . . I can avoid the BART.

Screw the train. If I'm stuck in this day, the money will magically reappear overnight in my bank account anyway, right?

Except I don't have a phone to call a cab. I glance up and down the block. There probably hasn't been a pay phone here in decades.

Sigh. Train it is.

When it lurches to a stop, instead of grabbing the pole, I grab the redhead in the bright clothes.

"*Excuse* me," she snips.

"Sorry." So not sorry. My hand is clean. I would never grab someone, normally, but my hand is too clean for me to care.

I walk briskly down the sidewalk toward the Blue Wave building.

Work is the same nightmare, except worse. I'm so flustered and befuddled that I have a hard time eking out more than a few clipped words to pitch the same old idea I already know they hate.

Of course the results are the same.

I would have fired me too.

Leaving the room, I make it two steps before Mark approaches with his trademark smile.

Panic stabs me in the gut, a cold and slimy blade. I *won't* do this again.

Spinning away, I bolt in the opposite direction, but not before his cocky smile turns into a confused frown.

The hallway leads to a back door and I open it, ending up in a narrow alley next to a dumpster.

I can't handle Mark today. Or any day. Definitely not sleeping with that guy ever again. I would rather jump in this stinking garbage than let him touch me again.

Just in case he follows me—though I doubt I'm worth the effort—I slip down the alley and stop where it merges into the sidewalk, leaning back against the brick wall to catch my breath.

I need to think. What do I do? How do I fix this? Why am I reliving the same day over and over and how do I get out of this . . . this *loop*?

Maybe I can fix my phone and call someone. But who?

My parents would be like, *Oh Jane, having a nervous breakdown. Again.* I don't need another lecture about all my problems and everything wrong with my life. All they want to hear from me is good news about being successful. Something I have yet to accomplish, really, which is why I avoid their calls.

I could call Eloise.

My sister. Maybe I could . . . no. I can't face her yet.

I have nothing else to do. But if I can get my phone fixed up, I can access the internet to research or something.

I take a train back to Emeryville and stop at the electronics store in the shopping center near my apartment.

"Can you help me fix my phone?" I ask the brunette woman behind the counter.

She tinkers with it, opening the case and pulling out the battery and trying different things I already tried yesterday that didn't work.

She puts a new battery in, but it still doesn't turn on. "Everything seems to be in order. Must be some kind of internal defect. We can order a new one to be shipped out overnight. You'll have it by tomorrow morning."

"Tomorrow morning," I repeat.

"Yes. That's the soonest we can get a replacement to you."

"Right." A giggle bubbles out of me. "Tomorrow would be great." I laugh. And then I can't stop. I'm laughing so hard, tears escape out of the corners of my eyes, and it turns into high-pitched cackling. The poor clerk glances around, probably wondering if anyone else is witnessing her customer dissolve into delirium.

This is exactly the scenario my anxious mind likes to concoct for me, when I have to go places and interact with people. *You're going to make a fool of yourself,* it tells me.

Well, here it is.

"I'm sorry," I finally say to the befuddled store clerk when I've pulled myself somewhat together and wiped my eyes. "Thank you. I'll leave now."

I leave the store, moving in the general direction of

my apartment, careful on the scarred and uneven sidewalk.

Now what?

I'm only a minute away from home, passing a row of shops I've walked by a thousand times, when I stop. And turn.

There's a store here, one I haven't seen before. It's possible I missed it, I guess. I don't get out much, and it's a small storefront shoehorned between a Thai restaurant and a dry cleaner.

The Druid's Stone, the sign reads in old English font.

Crystals hang in the window beside a little sign with a list. Candles, incense, tarot readings.

On autopilot, I open the door and a little bell dings, announcing my presence.

I glance around the narrow space devoid of people but cluttered with items. One wall is made entirely of dark wood shelves and stuffed with books. A mantel in the rear is lined with candles and repurposed wine bottles full of essential oils, labeled in script. The cash register on the counter in the middle of the space is old, made entirely of some kind of heavy ornate metal and shined up like polished silver. An ink pot with a feathered quill rests next to it. Patchouli mixed with sage and sandalwood infuse the air. It's like I've stepped into an apothecary from a hundred years ago. A cuckoo clock in the corner ticks the seconds. It's the only sound. The street noise is gone too. It's kind of eerie.

An arched doorway leads down a hall to another door—a windowed french door. Green is visible through the doors, like a garden is back there, but how can that be when the block is so narrow and there's an Ikea behind this building?

After a few minutes of glancing around, I wander over to the checkout and lean over the counter to get a better look at the register.

"Hello."

I jump and spin around. A young lady is right behind me. And I mean young. She can't be more than sixteen. She's wearing a Wonder Woman T-shirt and ripped jeans.

She's too close, in my bubble. I want to step back but can't since the counter is behind me. I'd have to step around her, but I don't want to be rude.

"Hi. Um. How do I get my fortune told?" I ask.

She stares, silent, a small smile on her face. The silence stretches and stretches. Can she speak? How can she stand there without moving or talking, not breaking eye contact? She doesn't seem uncomfortable with the quiet or the closeness.

Her head tilts as she considers me. "We don't do fortune telling."

I flinch with the sudden answer. "Oh, right. Well, then tarot readings?"

She stares at me.

"It said it on the sign." I point to it, even though it faces out the window and you can't read the words from here.

She neither confirms nor denies, her gaze unmoving from mine.

I fidget, having a hard time maintaining eye contact. This is why I hate talking to people. They're unpredictable. What is she thinking? Why is she staring at me? Is there something on my face? Shouldn't she be in school? Can she tell I've lost my ever-loving mind?

I can't handle the silence.

The clock in the corner ticks. Like it's a bomb about to go off and still, she stares.

"So. Um. Can I get some . . . tarot reading?"

She pauses again for so long, I think I'm going to have to repeat the question, but then she finally speaks. "Let me see if I can fit you in." She steps around me, going behind the counter.

I count out a quiet minute while she opens the dusty, leather-bound book and drags a finger down it.

She looks up. "It seems we're free. It's a ninety-seven dollars. Paid up front."

"Ninety-seven dollars?"

She nods.

I frown. That's oddly specific. Well, guess it doesn't matter anyway. I have some cash I'd been saving for a rainy day—which happens to be exactly ninety-seven dollars—tucked in a pocket of my wallet.

And well, it's raining. I used to have an even hundred, but I spent three dollars on a breakfast sandwich from a food cart the other week. Is it weird she asked for the exact amount I happen to have? I don't really want to give up my only cash, but I don't think the ancient cash register will take my credit card. Besides, what are my other options? What else am I going to do? I hand it over and she pulls a lever and tucks the money into the drawer.

Then she steps out from behind the counter. "Right through here."

I expect to be led to a dark room with candles, maybe to a table with a glowing crystal ball or something. But instead, she leads me through the arched doorway, down the tiled hall, and out into the garden.

Green vines weave over the muted red and brown brick walls enclosing the space. There's a miniature koi pond and fountain on one side, a stone bench overlooking them.

She motions for me to take a seat, so I sit, the cool stone leeching through my pants and chilling my thighs and butt.

She sits next to me. A little too close. I scoot as far over as I can without falling off the edge.

"Is there anything specific you are seeking guidance on? Any questions you want to ask of the universe?"

"Wait. Are you the psychic?"

Another lengthy silence. If her eyes weren't open, I might think she was sleeping. "I'm more of a spiritual advisor."

She's a teenager. What is she going to advise me on? TikTok and the rise and fall of Justin Bieber? This may have been the worst decision I've made on this day so far, and that's really saying something. But I doubt I'll get a refund. And I have no one else to talk to.

I think about how to phrase my question for a few seconds, to tell her the truth without coming off as completely unhinged, and finally settle on, "Every day is the same, over and over. And I have no control over anything. Do you know what I mean?"

She nods slowly, not meeting my eyes, instead looking out at the garden. I follow her gaze over the greenery to a statue of an angel perched on a concrete bust next to the pond.

She inhales and exhales a couple of times.

"Every day is the same," she repeats slowly. "Yes. It seems you have an issue with time."

My attention snaps to her, watching her profile. My breath catches in my chest. "Yes."

Her lips thin. Her head tilts. Then she shakes her head. "No. Time isn't your real issue. You just think it is."

"What do you mean? Time is the issue. It's exactly my issue."

She turns and meets my gaze head-on, unblinking. Then she grins. "Time doesn't exist."

"Oh," I laugh. "I beg to differ."

She shakes her head. "Time is not linear. It's more of a circle. But even that is too simplistic." She thinks for a minute and then snaps her fingers. "Time is like a taco."

"A taco?"

"You have something against tacos?"

"No. I love tacos. Especially the little street ones with the double tortillas, but how is time like a taco?"

"The tortilla is malleable. And you can fold it up to where one piece barely touches the other end.

Creating a kind of loop." She watches me, eyes narrowing.

My heart stutters. I didn't tell her I was stuck in a loop. How does she know? Or does she? Is this one of those phishing attempts where they are like, "You had an uncle with brown hair" or "You knew someone who died with a J name—John? Joe? Jerry?" and the dummy gasps and shouts "Javier!" and believes they're legit?

But at this point, can I really discount anything? I'm the one stuck in this damn time taco. "How do I get out of the loop?"

"You've been stuck for a long time. And now? You're only stuck because you think you are. You've been living behind a veil and the veil has been lifted. This isn't a trap you need to escape, it's an opportunity you need to embrace."

Frustration makes my jaw clench, my hands twist in my lap. "What does that mean?"

"It means," she spreads her hands out in front of her, "you're not stuck, you're finally free. Isn't it a beautiful day?" She leans her head back, as if feeling the sun on her face, but when I squint up at the sky, it's still foggy. Then she smiles again. "Sometimes life is as ridiculous as comparing time to a taco. Time is a construct. Past, present, future . . . these are things we've decided exist in some kind of order to try and force logic onto a more complex world. Minutes, seconds, days, years—humans created those concepts because we like to put things in their place. But reality, the here and now, is timeless."

I nod. I mean, I get it. And it sounds poetic and Buddhist and everything, but at the same time, philosophy can't help me get out of this damn Monday.

"Live in the now? Is that what you're saying?"

"I'm saying, focus on the things you can control and let go of the rest. You have today to have your tacos and eat them too. Does anything else really matter?"

Yes! Like living the rest of my life! She wants me to let go? Let go of what? I can't hold on to anything. I take a deep breath. "But what can I do then? To make things change?"

Her eyes meet mine, full of knowledge and something else. Peace. "Change is inevitable. But it doesn't matter. We all have to come to terms with the fact that we have no control over the world around us, regardless of the passage of time. Change isn't anything to fear. Change that happens around you doesn't matter. It's out of your control. There is only one thing we truly have power over."

"What is it?"

Her brows lift. "Ourselves, of course. If you truly want change, it starts with you. When you're on the right path, you'll know."

"How will I know?"

"Look for the signs. Trust yourself. You'll know."

Easy for her to say. I bet most of my signs will say "dead end."

"Okay." I blow out a breath. "That's great. I can change myself. Look for the signs. But that doesn't really answer my question. How do I get out?"

"The only way out is through, and the only way through is to love, Jane."

WELL, that was basically useless. The only way out is through, and the only way through is to love. Love who? What does that even mean? Does it mean I have to fall in love with someone? Or get someone to love me? In one day? I'm twenty-five and I haven't been able to get someone to fall in love with me in the two and a half decades of my life. Doing it in one day seems an exercise in futility.

I pace back and forth in front of my couch, wearing a path in the carpet, throwing my hands up periodically, and muttering to myself.

"I can control me." Great. What about everything else? Everything that happens to me, everything other people do to me? How do I stop all that?

I cease pacing and close my eyes.

There have to be some positives to this situation and I have to find them or I'm going to drive myself into . . . something worse than what I'm already experiencing.

List. I need a list. Lists put things in order. Being able to see it all written out in black and white, something I can control.

Grabbing a pen and small notebook, I sit on the couch and start writing.

What can I be grateful for?

I'm still alive.

I'm not in any kind of physical pain, only emotional.

I never have to pay rent again. Or any other bill. My bank account balance will revert back to normal each day—at least I think it will since I can't check it anyway. Should I write it down if it can't be confirmed?

Might as well.

I can do whatever I want and no one will remember the next day. I could go into work naked and it wouldn't matter. It would be like it never even happened.

I snort out a laugh. As if I could ever do something like that, even if it would be forgotten by everyone forever. I can barely handle talking in front of people fully clothed, let alone naked.

I want tacos. Food might help me think more clearly.

A couple hours later, I'm heading home with a bag of food and a crap ton of beautiful fabric I've been eyeing for months but was never brave enough to buy without risking homelessness.

And I found an old pay phone I had never noticed, back in the corner of the shopping center near the freeway. It was dirty and there was gum on the mouthpiece, but it worked. Tomorrow, if it's still Monday, I'm taking a cab.

I'm halfway down my block, almost to the front gate of my apartment, when a tall figure with sleek black hair emerges from the front entrance and turns at the sidewalk, heading in the opposite direction. Even from a distance, I know the stride, the set shoulders, the shiny hair.

Eloise.

My sister.

I don't call out. I don't say anything. I don't want to talk to her.

Not yet.

I glance at my watch. It's just after three. Now I know what time to avoid running into her.

Once she's disappeared, I head upstairs and eat my tacos, alone in the comfort of my familiar apartment.

Then I resume my endless thinking. And pacing. Thinking and pacing, while writing up a new ad idea for tomorrow. Something with love. If the child psychic says I need to get through this with love, that's what I'll focus on. Two lovers estranged, brought back together with the Splice app?

I scribble down notes, mind a whir of activity.

I'm going to fix this day. I'm going to come up with a new pitch and show them I can do it. That I have value. That I can fit. Maybe I'll even get to keep my job. Maybe I can keep going over and over until I get it right, figure it out. Maybe this is a chance from the universe to get what I want.

Or I'm dead and this is hell.

Or tomorrow, I'll wake up and it will be Tuesday and I'll just have ruined my own life by blowing most of my money on fabric, tacos, and teenage psychics.

I put all the fabric I purchased in the closet, along with some written ideas for a new pitch.

Tomorrow, we'll see what happens.

I lie in bed and try to think more positive thoughts. I can find a way to do something—take action. Like with the magic closet.

The neighbor is crying again. Muffled sobs. The soundtrack of my new life.

I pull a pillow over my head.

I have control of my choices and actions. I can get out through love.

The teenage psychic told me so. Spiritual advisor. Bah!

Except . . . disbelief wars with hope in my brain, a thought I've been avoiding all afternoon rising to the surface.

She called me Jane. I'm sure I never told her my name.

Chapter Six

SPRINKLE ME.

Well. It's Monday. Again.

And I need to check the closet.

I scramble out of bed.

The fabric is still there. The papers scribbled with new ad possibilities survived too. Everything I put in the closet survived the night. I turn around. Everything I didn't put in the closet is back where it was on the first Monday. The phone, the clothes, the briefcase . . .

It *is* a magic closet.

I spend ten seconds dancing around, my limbs a spastic blur divorced from the music's tempo, but whatever. *Something* is different, something I can maybe use to my advantage, and it makes me inordinately happy. I can control something in this weird . . . whatever this is.

I stop dancing and reconsider the confined space full of work clothes and boxes. Maybe I should sleep in the closet. It's small, barely large enough for me to sit in comfortably, but it might work. I'll try tonight. Something I can control, right?

I'll figure it out later. For now, I have to go get fired and then dumped by a narcissistic malcontent.

My stomach lurches.

I hate talking in front of people, and knowing I'm going to get fired at the end is like an extra turd on a giant crap cake.

But it's not a life-or-death situation like my mind wants to believe. Like my body seems to. My own thoughts make it worse. They always have. How do I escape my own self-defeating thoughts?

But what else can I do? I have to get through this, right? At least I have a brand-new pitch to try out.

And I have an idea on how I can avoid the train.

I bring sanitizing supplies to the pay phone on the corner, clean it off, and then call the yellow cab.

I arrive at the office ten minutes sooner than I would have if I had taken the train, and I'm poop-free.

It's already a better day.

This is totally going to work.

Instead of asking Hannah or Presley to tell the others I'm here, I go straight to the conference room. I miss running into Alex but, oh well, it's not like he'll notice or care.

And still, knowing how this ends, knowing I won't die or anything doesn't change my body's response. I'm sweating. Again. My heart is racing. Again. Black dots swarm the edges of my vision.

No.

I can do this.

This is just a meeting. I've been here before. But why does my body respond like I'm surrounded by black mambas?

Ugh. Get over this, Jane.

It's great. It's fine. I'm going to sweat like a pig and screw it up and I hope I do, I hope it's terrible, I hope they go all *Lord of the Flies* and band together and kill me.

I almost laugh at the thought, the ridiculousness of my thoughts dropping my anxiety down a notch.

What's the worst that can happen? It already has. They're just going to fire me. It sucks, but it's not death.

"It opens with a brief clip showing the development of a budding romance, two lovers meeting for the first time at a restaurant. More clips of them dating, kissing, moving in together, a whole relationship revealed in the span of seconds. Then they're fighting, yelling in the rain, at night. They're both alone.

"But then she's walking along the street near their first meeting. She gets a notification and he's there, at the restaurant they first met. They reunite, it's very romantic, and the tagline reads: a splice of life."

Blade and Drew exchange a glance. Did Blade roll his eyes?

Okay, maybe it's not the best pitch but I came up with it in the span of an afternoon, shouldn't that get me something? I thought it wasn't half bad. And it's about love. That's what's supposed to get me through this, right?

"Jane, it's fine, but it's not quite there," Stacey says.

I let out a breath. I know what's coming next.

"So, you're firing me." I deflate like a popped balloon.

"Don't think of this as a door closing. It's a whole bunch of new doors waiting to be opened."

"Right." I gather up my papers but then stop. "Wait." The last thing I want to do is extend this conversation, but I have to know. I force the words out, my voice quavering through it. "What could I have done differently?"

"We want something with more emotional punch. But I'm not sure you have it in you, Jane," Drew says.

Basically what they've already told me.

I leave and head straight out the back into the alley, avoiding Mark, avoiding Alex, avoiding everyone.

There has to be something I can do. Something that can adjust or shift or *something*. I will find a pitch that works, even if I have to work on it all day every day for a month of Mondays.

I am not giving up. I will change this one thing about this day if it kills me.

～

OVER THE NEXT however many Mondays, instead of working on keeping my job like I declared I would, I work on doing anything and everything I can think of to get out of it.

Having a panel of critical people staring at me and judging me and finding me lacking is . . . worse than having a mouth full of bees. I push through it, trying new things a half dozen times, but I need a break.

So I run some experiments.

First, with the closet. The magic closet only works for inanimate objects, and it doesn't work for everything. When I try to sleep in the closet anyway, I end up back in bed the next morning. Twice.

Most inanimate objects stay in the closet without disappearing, like fabric, papers, toiletries, books. Everything but money. Money and me seem to be the only things the closet spits back out overnight.

The universe wants me to be miserable and poor. There's my sign.

Attempting to stay awake all night doesn't work either. I black out from forces beyond my control at around five a.m. And it's a terrifying and sudden blackness. Not a fun experience, one I do not wish to repeat, so that one becomes a hard pass after the first attempt.

Leaving the city is impossible. When I go to the airport in the morning, the planes are grounded because of fog and low visibility on the runway, and there are no rental cars available. June gloom. Dammit, Karl.

I also go to a few different doctors. A neurologist first. They run tests—CT scans, blood work, an MRI— to rule out brain-tumor-induced hallucinations and any other physical cause. Everything comes back clean. As far as I know anyway, maybe they're part of the hallucination too. Who knows? Also, a majority of the tests don't have results for a few days. Ha. Yeah, "We'll call you tomorrow" always gets a good laugh.

I try a psychiatrist, but I've done therapy before for my anxiety and they want to schedule future sessions and prescribe medication.

So I'm stuck. Even if it's all a dream, it's one I can't get out of.

And the only way out is through. So time to choke on some bees.

"THE SCENE IS a crowded dance club. The camera fixes on a group of friends showing up together and having a great time dancing, but they get split up in the crowd. Both groups end up leaving. They need food after a long night, right? And then one group gets a notification that their other friends are at a restaurant nearby, and they find each other and eat together. The tagline can be: Splice up your life."

Stacey winces. "Well . . ."

"A splice of heaven?"

"No." Drew shakes his head.

"A FAMILY OVER THE HOLIDAYS, getting together, sharing the love, any way you splice it!"

The room is silent. Three sets of eyes staring at me.

Stacey smiles, but it turns into a wince. "Um. What exactly are we splicing?"

"THE GREATEST THING SINCE SPLICED BREAD."

Blade sighs, his pen tapping on his notepad. "Jane, the demographic that would recognize that cliché is not using mobile apps."

"GRAB A SPLICE OF THE ACTION!"

Drew frowns. "I'm not sure dinner could be considered action."

"And I don't think the client wants to spend ad money on explosions." Blade raises his brows at me.

"CGI may be too expensive, I'm afraid," Stacey adds.

"SPLICE it right up your pie hole!"

Stacey frowns at me. "Wait. Um. What?"

"Never mind. I'll see myself out."

AFTER TWENTY-ODD FAILED PITCHES, however, the sting aches less and less. My nerves and anxiety aren't quite as debilitating. They're still there. I can't imagine them ever going completely away, not with three people staring at me with their beady little judging eyes. I guess immersion therapy works somewhat though, because I keep screwing up, over and over and over, and gradually, I stop caring as much about their reactions.

Getting fired doesn't hurt nearly as much the fiftieth time.

And that's where my silver lining ends.

The Mondays continue and no matter what I say, over the course of weeks and weeks of Mondays, the results are always the same. I can affect some things, like how I get to work, who I talk to each day. I may be able to avoid getting poop on my hand and sleeping with Mark, but that's about it. I still get fired. Over and over and over.

The more days pass, the more I realize how vile he is. Why did I ever hook up with that jerk? Ugh. It makes me want to spew just looking at him now.

He is definitely not what this love thing is all about and if he is, the universe is messed up.

I want to let him know exactly what I think about how much of a repulsive, sickening, revolting turd he is. I have a whole speech planned out in my head, crafted over the course of so many Mondays, using a lot of adjectives, but despite the anger bubbling in my veins every time he's in my general vicinity, I can't do it. I try a couple of times. I open my mouth to tell him off and the words stick in my throat and my heart starts beating too fast, and I just can't. So I run away.

I try to stay positive, but frustration gets to me after getting fired for the zillionth time.

One Monday, after getting fired again and avoiding Mark by mumbling something about being on my period, I leave out the front for the first time in a long time, shoving open the door and exiting without looking back, my mind trying to drag me into the mire of depression.

What's the point of reliving the same day if I can't actually change the major outcomes, the things that made it so shitty to begin with? It's been almost three months of this now.

Footsteps pound the pavement behind me.

"Hey, Jane. You okay?"

"Alex. Hey. Yeah. I'm all right." I'm not but what can I do about it that I haven't already done?

"How did the pitch go?"

I shake my head. "Not great."

"Oh. I'm sorry."

Alex is among the things and people I've been avoiding. When I run into him, he's sweet and concerned and he asks about the interview and I brush him off. I don't want to admit I've been fired. It's embarrassing. Shameful. But I hate lying to him. He's always so honest and open about everything.

During his very first meeting with the marketing

team at Blue Wave, he talked about his failures, how many mistakes he'd made along the way to success. He said he learned more from failure than from success, and he didn't want anyone on his team to be afraid to fail, because fear prevents creativity.

I wish I could be more like him. Fearless in the face of adversity, instead of just a scared failure.

I could tell him the truth. I know him well enough to know he's not the judgmental type, but opening up to people, especially people I respect and admire, is like being skinned alive. Rejection and lack of under-standing is too common an occurrence.

And yet.

"I got fired," I blurt out. Heat fills my face. I can't meet his eyes, instead fixating on a crack in the side-walk. Why did I tell him?

"Oh, Jane. Hey." He dips his head to meet my eyes. "That really sucks."

I wave him off, even though my eyes are stinging. This is humiliating enough without crying in front of Alex. I'm a lot of things, but a crier isn't usually one of them.

Maybe because I usually don't talk to other people about my problems.

I shove the thought away. Now is not the time for introspection. "It's fine."

But it's not fine. I blink back the tears. I hate this day. Over and over this damn day.

"Hey listen, I'm in a band. We have a gig tonight. I mean, it's not a big thing, we're the opening act and it's at the Saloon, but you should come. I'll buy you a drink."

"Pity invite, huh?" I laugh, the sound brittle.

"No." He shakes his head. "Not at all. You should come. Please?"

Alex's expression is careful, his hands shoved into his jeans.

This is new.

This is different.

On the Mondays I don't avoid Alex, he never asks me to this show. I didn't even know he was in a band.

A normal person would jump at the chance. But of course, my first thought isn't about spending time with Alex. My first thought is about social anxiety. Go, by myself, to a bar I've never been to, to potentially hang out with Alex and his bandmates? Please. The old Jane would run so far and so fast, she'd leave a Jane-sized outline in smoke. I still want to say no. This is totally and completely outside of my comfort zone. I'll probably do something dumb or make a total ass of myself.

But . . . is this a sign?

And if there's no tomorrow, what does it matter?

Why *not* go?

It would be different. Different is good.

I need to change something about this day. And if I do something awkward and embarrassing, as I do, it's not like anyone else will remember because tomorrow will reset everything, so really, there's no risk.

I could show up wearing a G-string and cowboy

boots and the slate will wipe itself clean overnight like it never happened.

"Yeah. Maybe." I straighten. "I mean, I'll go." My voice shakes only a little.

His whole face lights up with his smile and I can't help but smile back, even if my lips tremble with the motion. "Really? That would be amazing. Eight o'clock."

I give him a shaky nod and straighten my shoulders. "I'll be there."

Chapter Seven

I'M GOING TO DO THIS. I AM. I'M GOING TO CHANGE something about this day and I'm going to go to this bar to watch Alex's band. By myself. Not knowing anyone. All alone.

The words pound through my head, each phrase ramping up my anxiety more and more the closer the train gets to my apartment.

What the hell am I thinking?

I can't go to a bar by myself. I can't even go to a bar with other people when I'm invited and I know them and have worked with them for years. The crowds. The smell. People watching me, wondering who is this loser at the bar alone.

And what about after? The thought of spending time with Alex outside of work sends a swarm of crows with razor-sharp talons winging through my stomach.

But the thought of showing up and *not* spending time with him is worse. What if he ignores me? What if he has a new girlfriend and she shows up too, and they both stare at me with pity and a vague sense of unease? What if he's only inviting me because he thinks I won't go?

After all, I was removed from Alex's team because of . . . I shut my eyes, but it doesn't stop me from hurtling back in time, to when I thought there might be something more between us. One more idiocy to add to the mile-long list.

"Did you get lost in here?" Alex asked one fateful day, coming up next me in the stock room.

I had gone to get paper to replenish the printer but decided to take a minute to catch my breath. We'd been working together alone for hours, and being the object of Alex's focus for long periods of time was invigorating, but trying not to say or do anything stupid was exhausting.

Not to mention fighting the ever-present attraction, a live wire that bounced around, shocking me in the heart every time he gave me a lopsided smile or touched my arm.

"Not lost. I'm just trying to, you know, pick the best one."

We stared at the identical stacks of packaged printer paper together.

He rubbed his chin, considering the options. "It is hard to decide."

"And what about the ones I don't pick. What if they feel left out?"

He snorted. "Like getting picked last for dodgeball, something that happened frequently to me in middle school. I feel for the paper, I do."

I groaned. "Dodgeball is the worst. It's torture. Who wants to be picked first for torture?"

He turned to face me, standing only a foot away, his eyes dark in the low light of the closet. "What if being printed on is torture for the paper? Must be painful. Stacked in a dark tray, yanked through gears and machinery, and forcefully covered in ink."

I laughed.

This was one of the many things I appreciated about working with Alex. I could talk to him about anything that popped into my head, even if they were completely random tangents. I could make ridiculous statements about paper feeling lonely and he would play along.

He reached for my face then, tucking a strand of hair back behind my ear. His fingers lingered on my cheek. His eyes dipped to my mouth.

Holy shit. Did he want to kiss me? Was this really happening? Was I dreaming? I wanted to pinch myself, but if this was real, there was no way I'd risk it.

I leaned into him and shut my eyes, every cell in my body gravitating toward him like he was a mirage in the desert, and let me tell you, I was thirsty. His breath caressed my lips, and then . . . and then he pulled away.

"Uh, here, I think this one is dying for torture."

I opened my eyes. He grabbed a ream of paper from the stack and left the room. Shocked, I stood there, staring at where he had been a moment ago. What had just happened? It took me a minute to collect myself. A long minute. When I went back to the employee area, we went back to work. Had I imagined the whole thing?

He acted like nothing happened. And then, the next week, I was off his team.

I'm sure he asked for me to be removed because of that moment with the paper. I, of course, spent weeks obsessing over it. What did I do wrong? Could he tell how into him I was and was embarrassed for me? Whatever he did, touching me, leaning in, he clearly thought it was a mistake.

I thought we were friends. We bonded over a shared love of colorful design. I even helped him pick the colors for different levels of Bubble Crush. That's when I told him about my own dreams of designing clothing. And he didn't laugh or tell me it was a pointless dream like everyone else. He didn't point out my drab work clothes and lack of visible style. He encouraged me. He sincerely appreciated my hidden creative streak. At least, I thought he had.

Shortly after that, Mark showed an interest in me and . . . he's not worth mentioning.

I get home and try to work on a new pitch, but I can't focus.

My resolve wavers about forty-seven times over the course of the day.

Figuring out what to wear is an agonizing decision. I want to look cool but casual, nice but not like I'm trying too hard, sexy but not overly so. I wish I could call Eloise or ask her advice, but the thought makes me queasy.

Besides, I don't have a phone.

I finally settle on a pair of dark, stretchy jeans and a T-shirt Eloise gave me. It's a multihued V-neck, colorful and vibrant and more eye-catching than I would like but there's a bit of red lace in the bottom of the V covering my slight cleavage, and I have a little red jacket to match. She wore it to some teen choice award. I think she wore it as a dress, but it barely covers my ass so I'm not sure how she managed to pull that off.

I use the dirty pay phone to call a cab and take it into the city, jangling with anticipation and unease the entire ride. I attempt to distract myself by gazing out the window as we drive over the Bay Bridge and into the city, the cables and towers dazzling in white lights, the city a glimmering jewel in the distance. But it doesn't help.

The cab drops me on the corner of Grant and Fresno, right in front of the Saloon. The building is two stories, with chipped and faded red siding.

There's no line to get in. I sort of expected one. I mean, Alex is pretty chill, but he is an up-and-coming millionaire. I've seen articles of him in *The Chronicle* regaling the locals about his successes and noting even who he's dating and where he's been spotted around town.

The battered wooden front door is open but I stop at the corner, staring at the words painted on the glass front window: *Saloon established 1861*.

Sounds filter out into the night, laughter, music, people talking, glasses clinking.

My stomach churns, my body thumping with the urge to flee.

No. I'm not running. I'm going to do this.

I force myself to move to the front door and peek inside. Despite the noise, it's only half full.

Thank the heavens. If it was packed, my willpower might have run away along with the rest of me.

The lighting is dim, which helps. If it's dark, people can't see me as clearly and therefore can't judge my every move and outfit choice. Most of the patrons are in jeans and tees. I tug on the hem of my fancy shirt, beelining to the dark wood bar and the first empty seat I can find.

I perch on a stool, avoiding eye contact with anyone and everyone—especially Alex, who is onstage with a drummer to back him up.

The setup is small, a raised platform in the back of the one-room bar. Along the wall opposite me is a long table lined with more barstools for additional seating.

Once I'm somewhat settled, I manage to swallow past my dry mouth long enough to order a drink from the bartender. A few chords strum through the room.

I swivel around in the stool.

Alex is wearing the same clothes from earlier. The drummer is dressed just as casually, T-shirt and jeans, and he has the biggest, most well sculpted Afro I've ever seen.

"Sorry, we're not as good looking as the Flight of the Conchords," the drummer says.

"And neither of us has a sexy accent." Alex strums the guitar along with his words.

"Also we aren't funny," his bandmate adds.

I laugh along with a few other patrons, the ones who are paying attention and not chatting or drinking.

"We couldn't even come up with a band name," Alex says.

"So we've decided to call ourselves Name This Band."

They segue into a song, a jaunty sea shanty about hats.

I wasn't sure what to expect, but it's not this. They aren't just a band, they're a comedy duo.

I sip my drink and take in the show, my focus almost entirely on Alex with only occasional glances at the drummer. Alex is so comfortable there, onstage, singing in front of strangers.

I could never do this.

The words of the song blur into the background as I fixate on his fingers, long and capable, strumming the strings. He can sing pretty well, actually. Even though the songs are simple and silly, his voice is a deep tenor, sending chills up my spine and then back down, spreading heat through my stomach, quieting the nerves in my belly. Apparently, I have a thing for musicians. Or it's just Alex.

They aren't getting rolling laughs from the small crowd, just the occasional chuckle and claps from the part of the audience that is actually paying attention. But they're clearly having a blast, exchanging grins, singing alone and together with perfect timing. Even though it's a small-time gig and they're singing about sombreros versus ball caps. They would be enjoying themselves if the room were empty. It's random and funny and their enjoyment is infectious.

I have so much fun watching and clapping along that when it ends, I'm jolted back to reality. I've been sitting here alone, actually enjoying myself. I almost forgot to be apprehensive about being somewhere on my own and surrounded by strangers.

Scattered applause breaks out across the bar. They bow and thank the audience, then Alex sets his guitar off to the side and steps off the stage.

Three women sit at a table on the side—leggy blondes with short skirts—and Alex and Leon head in their direction. One of them jumps up and gives Alex a hug.

Probably a girlfriend. I spin around in the stool, facing the bar, nerves that had settled during the show quivering back to life.

I clench my empty glass. My drink is gone. I should leave now, while I'm ahead.

He invited me because he felt bad, but I'm sure one of those women is his date. I'm just a friend. Not even that, more of an acquaintance. What if he comes over here and introduces one of them as his girlfriend? He'll be able to tell I've dressed up, put on makeup. Made an effort.

I'm hot and itchy. I should leave.

I slide off the stool, my toes barely touching the ground when a voice stops me.

"Hey." Alex's smile is bright and surprised, still flushed with adrenaline from the performance, no doubt. "You made it."

"I did." My voice is a little shaky. Maybe he won't notice over the hum of conversation permeating the space around us.

He's smiling at me, expectant, and I have no idea how to have a conversation with him outside of the office.

Oh, crap.

Tension grips my stomach in a tight fist. "The music —you did, I thought, um, it was really great. I know sea shanties are a thing, but I'm not sure I've heard one that's also, uh, comedy."

His eyes dip to my midsection, where my hands clutch my purse like a lifeline.

His smile droops. "Are you leaving already?"

"Yeah, well, I don't want to intrude on anything." I glance behind him, looking for the leggy blondes.

"You aren't intruding," he says quickly. "Just stay for a little bit longer? I said I would buy you a drink, remember?"

"Oh, um."

Anxiety whispers in my ear. *You're going to say something stupid. You have nothing to talk about. Nothing in common. He's going to think you're a weirdo. He probably already does. He feels bad for you and he's nice and now he's going to hate you.*

I want to run. I want to hide.

But I have to remember the whole point of this. At least, what I think is the point. I can control me. If I do or say anything dumb, he won't remember it anyway. I could jump up on the bar and yodel while beating my hands against my chest like an ape and no one would remember it tomorrow. Except me. And even knowing that to be the truth, it doesn't stop the fluttering of my heart or the sweat in my palms.

"Yes. Sure. A drink sounds great. Um. Gin and tonic."

He tells the bartender, ordering himself a beer, and we wait while the bartender gets our drinks. We stand side by side at the bar in silence. People jostle around us. More patrons file in through the front door.

Alex shifts toward me as more bodies crowd the bar.

He smells good. Like aftershave and soap. Simple. Clean. Much better than the cologne and beer filling the rest of the space. His scent is familiar since we've worked together and I've been this close to him before, sitting next to him in meetings and whatnot. But not like this. This is distinctly different.

We're not in the office, we're in a bar, having a drink together, and he's talking to me instead of one of the many women he could be talking to. My heart pounds in my chest, a heavy hammer of doom. He could be with anyone but me. Except he's not really *with* me. We're standing here in silence.

Crap. I need to make conversation. My mind blanks.

The bartender puts a glass in front of me and I take a few long sips through the little straw.

This is one of the many reasons I avoid socializing. I have nothing of interest to contribute. I hate small talk. Most of the things my brain lands on are lame or boring or weird, and people look at me funny or immediately have somewhere else to be, someone else to talk to.

Maybe that's why I'm reliving the same day over and over again. Even the universe is tired of my awkwardness and inability to have a normal interaction with another human being.

Say something! Anxiety spikes.

"Um. Well." I shove aside the straw and finish the drink in two long gulps. "Thanks for the drink. I have to go." I slip off the chair on the opposite side.

"Wait, Jane!" he calls.

But I . . . I can't do it. I weave around people, getting lost in the growing crowd, grateful for once to be surrounded by others so he can't easily find me.

Outside, I take deep gulps of the chilly night air, the cool breeze on my hot face a relief. I hurry down the sidewalk, arms wrapped around my middle like they might keep me from jumping out of my own skin.

Why can't I do this? Why can't I be normal? What

is wrong with me? Anger bubbles inside, threatening to explode.

I'm so sick of myself.

Routine. Control. Order. Those are the invisible clothes I wear every day. The ones that keep me from panicking, overanalyzing, or freaking out on a constant basis. Except it doesn't work. It never works. It's still there, like a tiger, waiting to jump out and attack at the worst possible moments.

You'd think reliving the same day over and over, having some kind of routine, would be a soothing occurrence for someone like me. I mean, I know what to expect. And yet, this day. This day . . . it's the worst. Why this day of all the days the universe could have stuck me in?

My footsteps quicken, slapping against the pavement.

I have no legitimate reason to panic about a simple conversation with someone I've known and worked with for months. Someone who will remember nothing of it tomorrow. And yet, it's like I can tell my brain those words over and over and it just won't believe it.

I hate my brain.

I make my way back across the bay to Emeryville. Somehow, I find myself in front of the Druid's Stone.

It's after ten, but light streams out of the windows, shining glowing squares onto the cracked sidewalk. And when I push on the door, it opens with ease.

"Hello?"

An illuminated lamp casts shadows over the space. The cuckoo clock ticks in the corner.

I sigh out a breath and shut my eyes. "What am I doing?"

When I open my eyes, she's standing right in front of me, only a foot away. "Holy mother of tacos!" I press a hand to my pounding heart. "You scared the crap out of me."

She's as still and immobile as a mannequin, wearing the Wonder Woman shirt and ripped jeans she had on the last time I was here.

Well, duh, it *was* the same day.

When my heart doesn't cease beating from her surprise appearance, I find my voice. "Hey. You're here. I didn't get your name last time."

Her head cocks to one side. "Last time?"

Oh, right. I guess part of me hoped she would remember, somehow.

I shake my head. "Uh, never mind. Are you giving readings right now? I know it's late but I thought maybe we could talk?"

She slips around the register and does the same thing as before, running a finger down the appointment book.

She looks up. "We're booked."

I glance around. "It's empty."

"I can't help you."

"Why not?" I motion at the door. "You're open."

"Now is not a good time. Come back tomorrow."

Frustration squeezes me in its grip and shakes.

"What do you mean? I need help. I need help now. I can't come back tomorrow."

But my exasperation doesn't affect her calm. "What you need is to help yourself. You don't need a reading. You know what you need to do. You're just not ready to do it."

Any argument I might voice dies on my lips.

She's right. I do know. Giving my pitch over and over, day after day, was brutal torture. But I did it. I got through it, more than once.

But this is Alex. I've been low-key crushing on him forever. I don't know how to get through this.

Which makes her even more right about that last bit. I don't want to do this. Because I'm scared.

But I'm sick of anxiety and fear. I'm sick to death of myself. Anger boils in my blood, filling every vein and crevice of my body. I'm *livid*. It needs to change. *I* need to change.

"What is it you want?" she asks.

I slump against the counter across from her. "For time to move forward."

"No, that's not what you want, that's what you think you want. What do you want?"

"I want to . . . I don't know, I want to know what to do? I want to make things right?"

She shakes her head. "Is that a question or an answer? *Why* do you want things to be right? What things? And what will making it 'right' do for you?" She lifts her fingers in air quotes.

"I just want," I shrug, "I want to be happy."

She nods and smiles, as if finally satisfied with my answer. "Time doesn't have anything to do with happiness. Time is outside. Happiness is inside. When you know what you want, the universe will conspire to bring it to you. You are the one pushing it away. You have to let it come. Do you see?"

"If I say no, will you explain it more?"

She smiles. "No."

Chapter Eight

ANXIETY IS LIKE WALKING THROUGH A DARK TUNNEL with no lights at either end. Except it's not even a real tunnel, it's an imaginary tunnel. You aren't actually in the dark, confined space, it just feels like it.

Even if you're out in the open air, all you can see is the darkness.

This is me. Trapped in a tunnel of my own making.

I know this. Logically, I know it's all in my head. I've gone to therapy, I've tried the pills, I've heard the theories and used the various tools to soothe the monster under the bed. But it doesn't make it go away. It doesn't make the fake monster any less real. The monster is still there, waiting to jump out and scare me as soon as I let my guard down.

I have to change me, and to get through this, that means I have to talk to Alex.

I think.

Either way, I'm going for it. I'm going to have a conversation with Alex and I'm not going to freak out and he's going to invite me to the show again and I won't leave, I'll be normal. I'll just talk to him. People talk every day. All the time. Most people can't shut up. I can be that person.

Footsteps pound the pavement behind me, thumping in time with my heart.

"Hey, Jane. You okay?"

I try to breathe through the nerves. "No. Not really."

"How did the pitch go?"

"It didn't go well at all. Terrible, actually. Really, really bad. Horrible."

I wait for him to invite me to his show. But he doesn't. He says, "I'm so sorry, Jane."

And that's it.

I stare at him. Waiting.

He glances back at the building. "You're leaving?"

"Yeah. I need to go home." I widen my eyes, lifting my brows, as if the motion might compel him to ask the question. Why isn't he asking? Didn't he ask yesterday when I told him it went badly? What else did I tell him? I try to remember but it's hard to think straight when my stomach is rolling and my knees are shaking.

"Do you need a ride?"

"No, I don't need a ride. I—" *I need you to ask me to your show.* The one I'm not supposed to know anything about yet.

My face heats. Nerves collide inside like pinballs in a

machine. The tunnel shudders and shakes around me. I can't panic in front of him, even if he won't remember it tomorrow.

"I-I gotta go. Bye."

I walk away, confusion thrumming through me. I need to calm down and think. Why did he ask me yesterday and not today? Or any other day, for that matter? Yesterday was the first time he invited me. My steps slow. He only invited me when I told him—"I got fired!" I blurt out, spinning around, ready to march back and tell him.

But he's already gone.

～

"HEY JANE, YOU OKAY?"

"No. I got fired." The words are quick and high pitched and loud. An embarrassing gunshot of words. *Gah, I annoy myself sometimes.*

His mouth pops open in shock. "Um. You. What?"

I guess I'm not usually so forthright. Or shrill.

My face heats. My nerves spin around in my stomach like I'm stuck on a wonky carousel from hell. The tunnel is collapsing.

Dammit.

I open my mouth. Close it. Open it again. Close it. Ugh. Spinning on a heel, I flee.

～

"HEY JANE, YOU OKAY?"

Play it cool, Jane. I've been practicing. It's a script now. I can do this.

"I'm," I clear my throat, "not great. The pitch didn't, um, it didn't go good."

I could never be an actor. I can barely speak. I'm like the animated version of the children's books written with my namesake. See Jane run. See Jane fail. See Jane pull her tongue out and stomp on it for all the good it's doing her.

"What happened?"

"I got fired."

"Oh, Jane. Hey," he dips his head to meet my eyes, "that really sucks."

"Yeah." I sigh and look into the distance, giving it my best thousand-yard stare. *Be forlorn. So sad. So, so sad you should invite me out. Don't I look like I need a night out?*

"Hey listen, I'm in a band. We have a gig tonight. I mean, it's not a big thing, we're the opening act and it's at the Saloon, but you should come. I'll buy you a drink."

"Yes. Oh, um. I mean, yeah, cool. Maybe. Maybe I'll see you there." I back up slowly.

Walk away before you screw this up somehow.

I spin around to stalk off.

"Eight o'clock!" he calls after me.

And I'm very glad I turned around before he could catch the full-on grin stretching my face. I did it! I wave a hand behind me in acknowledgment and keep walking.

Time to prepare.

I spend the rest of the day coming up with a list of things to talk about. I don't know why I haven't done this before. Lists are my jam, my go-to strategy almost every time I have to talk to people, or in front of a group. I use them for everything. Make a list, memorize it, repeat it over and over so I can hopefully speak through my nerves without stuttering too much, or sounding like a complete dolt.

I sit in my living room with my notebook and brainstorm.

I can ask him about the band, how he got started, why there's only two of them . . . Wait, is that an offensive question? What if it's because they suck and can't get anyone else? I mean, they seemed good to me, but what do I know? I cross it out.

I can ask about his family, maybe? Is that boring?

I suck at this.

I definitely don't want to talk about work. I tap my pen on the notebook, thinking.

Maybe I can ask if he has any other late-night hobbies? Oh wait, that might come across as sexual. *Late-night* hobbies, wink wink.

Just ask about hobbies, minus the late-night bit. Any hobbies other than playing guitar. I write it down. I could ask where he got his guitar, when he started playing guitar, how long he's been playing guitar . . . I write those down and look over my list. He's going to think I'm obsessed with guitars.

Okay, Jane, it's not a big deal. You won't be the only

person there, he will be talking and asking questions too, right? I can't be responsible for all aspects of interactions. I've had plenty of conversations with Alex, but we were also working together so there was always a fallback topic.

And that first night, he didn't say anything either.

Maybe he was nervous too?

I chuckle. No way. Nervous? Why would he be nervous? It's just me. Just plain ol' Jane. And he's Alex Chambers. *The* Alex Chambers.

Nervous crows turn into pterodactyls in my stomach and I have to focus on my breathing.

I can do this. I'm going to do this, every night, until I can have a normal conversation without panicking. No reason to fear. After all, there is literally no tomorrow.

I SIT at the bar in the same spot as last time, sipping my drink, smiling at the music, and going over the list in my head.

When their set ends, he jumps off the stage, just like before. I avert my gaze from the leggy blondes.

A half a minute later, he's next to my barstool. "Hey. You made it."

"I did. Thank you for inviting me." I smile through my nerves.

We go through the same motions from the night before as he orders our drinks.

When the bartender puts my drink down, I give a nod of thanks, take a long sip, and then force a few shaky breaths in and out. I can do this. I'm not running away. I am going to ask him questions. I am prepared. But as I'm opening my mouth, he speaks.

"I'm really glad you made it. I'm surprised you," he glances around to confirm, "didn't bring Mark with you? What did he think about you getting fired?"

"Mark?" I couldn't be more shocked if he asked me why I didn't bring a bright pink dancing flamingo with me.

My face heats. What does Alex know about Mark? What has he heard? Did Mark say something to him? I'm mortified at all the possibilities. The things Mark might have said. The things Alex might now believe.

Apprehension threatens to blast through my skin and paint us all in tension. I can't let my anxiety tell me what it thinks. I need to find the truth, not my mind's own terrible version of a false reality. Maybe a false reality. Please be a false reality.

Focus on the conversation, Jane.

"Oh. Him. Yeah. No. I didn't bring him and he doesn't know. He's not—we're not—we're not together. We're not even friends, really."

His mouth pops open, brows lifting in surprise. "What?"

"Did he tell you something about me?" I don't want to know but I have to know. Maybe the truth will be better than my imagination. I hold my breath, waiting for his response.

He shrugs. "Not really. He——" He considers me for a second, and I might run away now, before he can tell me something awful, but then he comes to some sort of internal decision. "I may have asked him about you, one night when the office went for drinks at Tunnel Top. He made it seem like there was something going on. Something between you two."

Surprise pierces through the thick layer of fear cloaking me. "Wait. You were asking about me? Why?"

My mind can't quite grasp it. Before Alex can answer and I can work it out, we're interrupted.

"Alex!" His bandmate is there, slapping him on the back and grinning at me. "Introduce me to your friend."

"Leon, this is Jane. Jane, Leon."

Leon's bright smile grows impossibly wider. "Oh, this is Jane? I've heard a lot about you."

"You have?" I shake his hand and lift my brows at Alex. He's talked about me?

Alex flushes slightly and looks away and my heart flips in my chest. What does this mean? What has he said? Did he tell him about the closet? Was he like, *I had to invite this sad woman Jane to our show tonight because she's lonely and pathetic and I'm the type to bring lost puppies home?*

The music starts, the next act taking the stage, and conversation is forced to a halt.

"Let's dance!" Leon yells. Without waiting for any kind of response, he struts out to the extremely tiny space for dancing and jumps around to the music, all by himself. It's pretty awe-inspiring. And he's actually quite good even though . . . is that the sprinkler?

"Can we talk, outside?" Alex leans into me, speaking into my ear.

I nod and follow him, weaving through people coming in to head outside onto the street.

We're at the top of Telegraph Hill. Behind Alex, Coit Tower is lit up like a giant concrete beacon against the stark night sky. A guiding light or a warning?

"I have to tell you something, and I really hope you won't hate me."

I swallow. Nothing good could ever follow that statement. I don't want to know, but at the same time, I have to ask. "What is it?"

He takes a breath, his eyes searching mine for a moment before he speaks. "It's my fault they moved you from my team. I asked for you to be transferred."

Harsh blow. I swallow. I knew this, or I guess I assumed. Having it verified is . . . Why is he telling me this?

Is this where he tells me how embarrassing it was when I thought he was going to kiss me? Also, he just likes me as a friend and please stay away from him now? He invited me out here to, what, point out my awkwardness? Hand over a restraining order? Couldn't he have done this earlier today?

He's still speaking. I struggle to focus on the words through the rush of blood in my ears.

"It wasn't because you weren't doing a great job,

you were. And it's not that I don't like you, but because I do."

I open my mouth. Shut it. Open it again. What is he talking about?

"Remember, that day, in the storage room. We were joking about paper and dodgeball?"

After a few seconds, I nod, unable to force words out.

"I backed off not because I didn't want to kiss you, but because I did."

The roaring blood in my ears freezes, the world gone silent. Wait. What? My mind scrambles, attempting to make sense of his words. "You . . . made me feel like an idiot because you like me?"

He winces. "I never meant to make you feel bad. I know it sounds horrible, but it wasn't fair to you. I'm a client, and I didn't want you to feel obligated, you know? I was basically your boss on the team, which makes it an imbalanced power structure and I really didn't want to put you in that position. So instead, I did something stupid. I pushed you away, and then I did something selfish and asked for you to be transferred from my team."

I can't figure out what he's saying. I mean, I under-stand the letters and the meanings of the words, but it's not computing.

"I don't understand. You ran away and then had me moved off your team because you like me? But you never said anything. Even after you . . . traded me off."

My voice is rising, anger overpowering the normal nerves.

How could Alex do this? I liked him. I trusted him.

Is he why I got fired?

He holds up his hands. "I was going to say something. I wanted to ask you to dinner or something sometime," the words come out in a rush, "but then Mark told me you guys were seeing each other."

I blink. Wait. The timeline isn't gelling in my mind. For one, Mark himself told me we aren't a thing even though we've been sleeping together for the past month, and for two, we weren't sleeping together when I was transferred from Alex's service. In fact, around that time was when Mark started hitting me up with the heavy flirting.

Wait a minute. Did Mark only take an interest because of Alex? Holy shit. Mark started hitting on me *after* Alex asked him about me, like I'm a shiny toy and he's a toddler, only interested when someone else wants to play with me. Which is just douchey enough to make sense.

Alex keeps talking when I don't respond. "And now, I feel like an even bigger fool because you just told me you and Mark aren't a thing. Weren't ever a thing. Either he was lying, which fits with his bigger picture, or . . . ?"

I rub my head. Is he serious? "He, *we* weren't ever serious. We may have—" My eyes fall shut. This is mortifying. "We may have had some physical moments. But it started a couple months ago and ended . . . well, today. And it was never, he never really liked me, like that."

His jaw tightens. "Mark's an ass. I'm sorry. I really hope that my asking for the transfer didn't have anything to do with you getting fired today. I was very clear to Drew you were an excellent employee. But I can call them and make sure, if you want. Not that you need me to fight your battles, but I feel really terrible that I might have had something to do with it."

I shake my head. "I don't think so. I—" I blow out a breath. "I'm not sure."

You don't fit, doesn't exactly mean *Alex likes you and therefore you're fired*.

I mull over everything I know about this day, the number of times I've been fired, the different questions I've asked, ideas I've tried at work, and I come to an inescapable conclusion. As much as I would love to deflect and blame someone else, I got fired not because of Alex, but because of me.

"No. It's not your fault. It's mine. You're not the idiot. I'm the idiot."

"So." He tips his head down, nudging the tip of my shoe with his. "What would you think about being idiots together?"

I laugh. Our eyes lock. His wry smile sinks into a more thoughtful expression. His eyes darken. His gaze drops to my mouth. My entire body flashes hot and my stomach squeezes tight. Is this really happening?

"Jane." He steps closer, into my space, forcing me to tilt my head back to hold his eyes.

His head dips down. This is incredible. Amazing. Fantastic. I stretch up. We're so close, his breath feathers my lips.

Oh, no. I'm going to screw this up.

Panic pushes up from the ground, starting at my feet and racing to the top of my head in a gush of dread. At the last minute, I wrench my head to the side and his mouth connects with my ear.

"Oh." He shifts back. "Um. Jane? I'm sorry, I thought—"

"No. I'm sorry. I-I—" I take a deep breath, or attempt to, but panic is a set of muscled arms wrapping around my chest, squeezing. I can't breathe.

Black spots cloud my vision.

Not this. Not now, of all times. Roaring fills my ears with white noise and my vision blackens. "I have to go."

Chapter Nine

I think Alex follows me, or tries to, but I lose him, passing through a busy crowd of people forming in front of the Saloon. My surroundings are a blur of streetlights and buildings and traffic and pedestrians. I focus on my steps, one at a time, something to focus on while I work to calm my galloping heart.

I keep going, on and on, until I can breathe again and the panic subsides. I've walked half the damn peninsula, chugging up and down hills, before my body settles down.

What is wrong with me? Why did I run from Alex? He tells me he likes me and we nearly kiss and I bolt? This is something I want, isn't it?

I like Alex. I like him more than he could possibly like me. And instead of reveling in a win for once, I push it away.

Why does my body fight me at every turn?

I *say* I want to be happy. I *think* I want to be happy, but when potential happiness is standing right in front of me, I flee like it's going to chew me up, spit me out, piss on me, and then set me on fire.

I stop next to a Buddha statue and glance around. I'm in a park. The Japanese Tea Garden. Lanterns are set every few feet, glowing soft circles of light over the bushes, greenery, and rocks. But most of the park is a blob of black in the darkness. I've been here before, with Eloise. It's pretty at night. But dark. I shiver and tug my jacket closer.

This place usually closes at five. And it costs to get in during the day. How did I get in here?

I frown at Buddha. Who knows? Magic tea garden, I guess.

My legs are tired. I plop down on the walkway and stare up at Buddha. He's sitting in the lotus position, the ornate circle of metal around his head etched with a flowery pattern. One of his hands is lifted, palm facing me, fingers curved. The other is near his lap, palm facing the night sky. He looks so peaceful. So sure of himself.

The universe is shoving happiness in my face and I'm the one blocking it out. The psychic teen was right.

Why do I do that?

I don't deserve happiness, so even as I want it and crave it and desire it, I run away from it. I'm not good enough. Never good enough.

You're not trying hard enough.

You can't make a living with costumes.

You need to set realistic goals, like Eloise did.

I'll never live up to my parents' expectations.

So then why do I keep trying? I should just do whatever I want, right? But they aren't wrong about everything. I need a job to live.

I blow out a breath. I can't think about my future career until I can get to tomorrow.

And I won't be able to make time move forward unless I get "through it with love" or whatever. I'm already a slave to this time loop. I can't continue to be a slave to my anxiety on top of that.

Maybe if I do this, pursue this thing with Alex, time will go on. If I open myself up to it all, good and bad. Love and rejection. Is that why I run from good things? Because if I get them, I'll find a way to screw them up?

Fear. It's my own fear, my own fake tunnel holding me back from everything.

The brain telling me I'm in danger when I'm not.

I'm taking control back, and it starts now.

"I HAVE to tell you something, and I really hope you won't hate me."

Even knowing in advance about this entire conversation, and where it leads, what's going to happen, I'm jittery and ready to bolt.

My responses are different though, now that I know

everything he's going to say and have had the luxury of thinking through the whole thing. Each time now, our conversation veers in slightly different directions.

And I keep getting stuck in my head and trying to calm myself down, which leads to silence, which leads to Alex speaking before I can get a word out.

"I'm not doing this right. I really just wanted to ask you to dinner, or coffee sometime or something?"

My tongue is thick, stuck to the roof of my mouth. I've already gone through this. *Just say yes, Jane.*

"Here's where you tell me you like me too, and you want to hang out sometime. Or you tell me to get lost. One of those."

"I do." Wait, that sounds like we're getting married. "I mean, I like you too, Alex. I'm definitely not telling you to get lost." I'm flushed. Overheating. With nerves or exhilaration, it's a combination of all the things.

My voice is high and squeaky. I can't believe I'm saying this to his face. Doubt pinches at me with crab claws. What if he goes "ha, sucker!" once I get these words out? I shake my head, like that will shake away the doubt. "I guess I'm having a hard time understanding why you would want to . . . drink coffee or eat in my general vicinity."

"Why wouldn't I?"

"Uh, because I'm a neurotic mess who can barely hold it together and you're . . . you."

His head tips to one side. "You don't give yourself enough credit."

"I don't think that's my problem."

His brows lift and he huffs out a laugh. He watches me for a second, considering. "Do you remember when we first met?"

"Of course. When you hired Blue Wave to help you market Bubble Crush and you came in to talk to the staff and pick your team."

"Right, but do you remember before the meeting started?"

"I remember." He'd been alone, in the hall where the bathrooms are, slumped against the wall, pale, sheened with sweat. I recognized the signs of a panic attack and talked him through some breathing exercises until he was calm enough to join the meeting. I've had some of those moments myself.

"You had no idea who I was."

I shrug. "I thought maybe you worked for Alex Chambers, not that you were *the* Alex Chambers. I expected some slick guy in a suit and you were wearing, well, something a lot like this actually." I use my free hand to motion at his faded Led Zeppelin tee.

He puts a hand to his chest, his mouth dropping open in mock surprise. "This isn't slick?"

"I mean, it's something."

He laughs, then hesitantly reaches for me.

I glance down.

His fingers engulf mine, long and graceful, artist's fingers, even though he's an app developer who plays mediocre guitar.

"I never explained to you what happened that morning."

"You don't have to tell me anything."

"I know I don't. But I want to."

He takes a deep breath, as if bracing himself. Maybe he's married. Maybe he's an alien. Maybe I need to stop talking to myself in my head and pay attention.

"When I was a kid, I had cancer."

This is not what I was expecting. "Oh. Alex." I squeeze his hand. "I'm sorry."

"It's fine. I mean, I'm fine now. It was acute lymphoid leukemia. It has a high survival rate, one of the less aggressive forms of the disease. But I still have to get tested every year, to make sure it hasn't come back."

I suck in a sharp breath. "Are you okay? Did it come back?" Is that why he was panicking? That was six months ago.

Holy shit, is he dying?

"I'm okay. I'm fine. But it's always there, you know, in the back of my mind. Will it come back?"

"How did I not know about this?"

"It's not something I share with anyone except my closest friends. And I was a minor, so it's not like it's public knowledge."

I'm still absorbing the fact he shared something so personal with me, something he hardly tells anyone, when he keeps talking.

"No one is digging up my dirt much to care at this point. Besides, I didn't want to use my cancer story to succeed. I wanted to do that on my own merits, you know? But every time I go and get tested—like I did that morning—I freak out a bit. And my point is, I guess, I understand what it's like to feel out of control of your body, and it's nothing that makes you any less worthy than anyone else. If anything, it makes you stronger."

I shake my head. "Freaking out over cancer is normal, expected. I never had cancer. I have no reason to be afraid all the time. You do so many things without fear. You came into Blue Wave that first day, and even after the hallway incident, you walked in there and told all of us all about your failures. Total strangers, you just admitted all your mistakes like it was nothing. And in there," I tilt my head in the direction of the Saloon, "on stage. I could never do that."

"Sure you could."

I give a short laugh. "You act like you've never seen me present in meetings."

"Everyone gets nervous in front of a crowd. Including me. You hate talking in front of people, and you don't like being the center of attention, but the important part is that you do it anyway. We have that in common. You think it makes you weak, but I think it makes you strong."

If only he knew how long it took me to even brave this conversation. "I can't believe you get nervous in front of a crowd. You do it with a lot more finesse and a lot less sweating." I grimace.

He laughs and steps closer. "How's the sweating right now? Is it okay?"

I shake my head. "It's dubious at best. Subject to change at a moment's notice."

"I think I'll risk it." He takes another step in my direction. "And if I were to, say, ask you to dinner sometime or something, you would say . . ."

I laugh. "That's very subtle. I would say yes. Definitely yes."

He squeezes my hand. I stare down at our linked fingers. Am I floating? I must be floating. I can't feel my head. Or my legs. My whole body is made of air. This is so surreal.

I take a breath and then one of his hands lifts to my cheek, tilting my head back. His lips brush against mine, a soft slide of pressure. He pulls back to look into my eyes.

His hand releases mine to cradle the other side of my face. He smiles once, a quick movement, his whole face alight for a blink of time, and then he's kissing me again and holy crap he is good at this. His lips are warm and soft, but unrelenting. He kisses like he does everything else, with confident abandon, forcing my complete surrender. When his tongue brushes against mine, my insides turn into goo and my knees get weak. His arm moves around my waist, pulling me closer.

I don't have any time to worry about my lips being chapped or my breath smelling like booze or any of the things I normally fret over because my mind is full of Alex. Only him. His smell, his fingers on my waist, the firm warmth of his body pressed against me. I push closer, craving more, needing all of it. His hand is a tender pressure on my face, fingers tracing my cheek. My arms are trapped between us and I pull them out, with every intention of wrapping them around his neck, but instead I accidently knock him in the chin with the backs of my hands.

He jerks back.

"Oh gosh, I'm so, so sorry." Heat floods my face. I'm sure I'm bright red. I've ruined this magical moment.

He's stunned for a second and then he laughs, exposing the strong column of his throat.

"Jane." He leans his forehead against mine, still chuckling. "Don't worry, it's perfect." Hot breath puffs against my lips, his mouth only inches from mine, a tempting torment, but then he pulls back. "So, dinner? Tomorrow?"

"Sure."

It's not perfect. Our first kiss and I punched him in the face.

But the bright side is I get a redo.

THIS TIME, I'm ready. I keep my hands at my side so when he leans in, I immediately raise them to his shoulders, sliding up to his neck as his mouth hits mine.

It's just as magical as before. More magical, since the threat of punching him in the face has been eliminated—for now.

I can't believe I'm actually kissing Alex. Alex! Even in my deepest, most secret fantasies, wishing for him to be mine was like wishing to become a superhero, or that I could eat nothing but carbs for the rest of my life and not gain a pound, or for the existence of an incorruptible society.

This has to be what will get me through this day and on to the next. Granted, a kiss isn't love. But his kiss is . . . everything. His mouth incites a riot of need. His hands generate waves of desire that coil around me in a tight vise of want. His body pressed against mine triggers a rush of uncontainable heat. Nothing in my limited experience compares to this kiss.

I drop my hands and wrap them around his waist, wanting to be impossibly closer. We share air, breathing together, his hands curved around my neck, tilting my head to the side so he can linger and nip at my bottom lip. I groan into his mouth, desperate for more.

A wolf whistle breaks through the lust haze, and Alex pulls back as people step around us, laughing.

Breaking apart, we stare at each other, breathing heavily.

Oh. Right. We're standing in the middle of the sidewalk on Grant Avenue.

He leans in again, hands gripping my waist. Then he rests his forehead against mine.

"So. Dinner? Tomorrow?"

Chills weave up my spine, driving away the desire burning me up only moments ago.

"Dinner. Tomorrow," I agree. Because what else can I do? There will be no dinner tomorrow. But the knot in my chest lightens a little. There might not be dinner, but there will be another first kiss, and that is something to look forward to.

Maybe this isn't such a terrible day to relive after all.

Chapter Ten
========

"SPRINKLE ME."

I wake up with a smile, rolling over to scream into my pillow. Wow. Yes. I can do this again. I can get through this terrible day, knowing what awaits me at the end if I play my cards right.

I can't get over the idea that he would pick me, *me*. I never would have imagined.

My mind runs over our every interaction, from our first meeting to every conversation and nuanced look, every subtle touch . . . all things I ignored because it was so farfetched. Then the moment together in the closet that wasn't. I just knew he took off because I was awkward and ridiculous. But I was wrong. I was so sure he had me removed from his team because he was uncomfortable around me. But I read the situation completely wrong.

Maybe my luck is changing. Maybe things will be different now.

"Jane, you just don't fit."

Then again, maybe not.

Okay, so not *everything* will be different, but being fired hurts a whole lot less knowing I get to make out with Alex later.

It's hard to play it cool around him. Not that I've ever played anything cool in my life. I can't stop grinning when I see him after my latest firing.

"I got fired!" I've never been so happy to admit to failure in my life.

A surprised laugh. "Is that a good thing?"

"Oh." I force my smile down. I can't let him know I'm happy, what if he doesn't invite me to the show? "It's terrible. I'm not happy."

"You're not?"

"I'm very depressed." I suck at subterfuge.

"Well, since you clearly need cheering up, you could come check out my band? We're opening at the Saloon. I'll buy you a drink."

Cool. Play it cool, Jane. "Yes."

His brows lift. "Yes? It's that easy."

I laugh, unable to stop the bubble of joy careening through me. I want to kiss him again. Now. But what if I make it mega weird and he changes his mind?

My smile droops.

He's going to think I've lost my mind.

"I'll see you later." I run away before I can do something stupid like throw myself at him and ruin the only good thing that happens on this godforsaken Monday.

"I WISH you had said something to me before." Before today. Then maybe we would have had a chance to go on that first date. Instead, I'm destined to stand here, outside of the Saloon every night, listening to Alex apologize for moving me from his team over and over again before we can get to the good stuff. Not that I'm complaining.

He rubs his chin. "I thought you were with Mark. And honestly, I thought you knew."

"How could I have known?"

"I thought you'd notice that I've been showing up at Blue Wave even when I don't need anything."

My brows lift. "You have?"

"Well. Yeah. At this point, everything could be handled with a phone call or delivered by a courier." He shakes his head. "Do you have any other clients hanging around post-production three times a week?"

I laugh. "I guess not. I never really thought about it."

"I can't believe you didn't notice. I thought I was so obvious."

It's pure greed inducing me to ask. "You came in just to see me?" The thought makes me all fluttery. I still can't believe it.

"Is that so surprising?"

I nod. "Yes. Actually. It is."

"Why?" His brow furrows.

"I'm me and you're you."

He shakes his head. "You need to give yourself more credit."

"I guess."

He steps toward me, his hands coming up to my face. "Now that we're on the same page, if I were to, say, ask you to dinner sometime or something, you would say . . . ?"

I grin. "Yes. Of course, yes."

He steps closer again.

And it's just as breathtaking as before.

He kisses me like he's been waiting to kiss me for months. It's tentative at first, slow and savoring. His hand comes up to my jaw, tilting my head just so, and then the kiss morphs from sweet and sensual to an exploratory seduction. His tongue slides against mine and a blast of burning desire surges through me.

I wrap my arms around him, tugging him against me, needing to be closer, persuading him with tongue and lips and teeth.

The whistle sounds again.

We break apart, the group of laughing people walking around us. Alex tugs me back against him, his head resting against mine.

"Wow." The word is a tickle on my lips and we take a minute to catch our breath. "So. Dinner? Tomorrow?"

My hands clench around his waist. "Yes. Tomorrow."

"WOW." He pulls back to rest his forehead against mine while we catch our breath. "You're really good at this."

"Uh-huh. Don't stop." I pull him back into me.

"JANE." His eyes search mine. "I have to tell you something, and I really hope you won't hate me."

"Alex. I know." I step into him.

"Jane, I—"

"Yes. Same. I get it. I like you too. Please kiss me."

Every night, we kiss. And kiss and kiss. And it's never enough. I'm constantly starved for more. More of him. More of his mouth on mine, his hands skimming my waist, being able to touch him anywhere. Well. Almost anywhere.

I press myself against him, and he slows us down to gentle pecks and touches and then breaks us apart to ask me to dinner.

AND AFTER THREE WEEKS, or more, I don't know, time is starting to slip away, the anticipation and discovery and inferno of desire are turning into . . . desperation.

Every night I get hot and bothered and every night, Alex wants to take me to dinner. Tomorrow. Dinner. Tomorrow.

Tomorrow doesn't exist!

I'm so horny, I can't sleep. Eating becomes an erotic event. My eyelashes are turned on.

I wake up wanting him. All day needing him. Every night with him and still, we kiss.

I want him more than I thought was physically possible, and I know he isn't immune, I've felt the proof of his arousal up close and personal. But for him, it's always the first kiss. And when I even try to push the boundaries, I get shut down. Understandably. We haven't even dated and Alex is . . . Alex. He wants to wait because he cares. I can't fault him for that.

Self-induced orgasms help at first, but it's not the same.

Alex is a gentleman in the truest sense of the word, and it's one of the things that makes him so attractive. I don't want him to change, but at the same time . . .

He wants to take me to dinner. He wants to woo me. He thinks we have the potential for something special and we can't ruin it.

But I think I might incinerate from the inside out if we don't push it to the next level.

"SO. DINNER? TOMORROW."

I grit my teeth together.

Tomorrow. Everything is always tomorrow. I hate tomorrow!

I take a deep, calming breath. Love. I need to get through this with love. I need to take control of myself. Not everything is about sex. I need to remember why I liked Alex in the first place, and it's not just because of his clever tongue and strong hands and leanly muscled physique.

Wait a minute. "Why don't we go now?" My voice is more clipped and forceful than I intended it to be.

His brows lift. "You want to go to dinner now?"

"Sure, why not? A lot of places are open this late." Plenty of people eat dinner late at night. People who work late, drunks, swing-shift workers, and lusty women stuck in time loops. There are no rules.

He shrugs. "I'm not hungry."

"You don't have to eat. Or we could get dessert. Or you could watch me eat." Because that's not weird.

He rubs my arms. "Jane, are you all right?"

"I need sustenance. Hunger is making me loopy." Ha. Loopy. Interesting word choice. And it fits. If I was one of the seven dwarfs, that would be my name. I shove away the ridiculous thought. Can constant arousal make you senseless?

"Well, then. Let's go eat."

Chapter Eleven

I SHOULD BE NERVOUS. I MEAN, I AM NERVOUS, BUT I should be more nervous.

I'm on a date with Alex. A *date* with *Alex*. Old Jane would have been freaking out, frozen, stuttering, possibly sweating all over the place, gassy, you know, the attractive stuff.

Now I'm new Jane. New Jane has made out with Alex more times than she can count on her fingers and toes. New Jane is more concerned with getting into Alex's pants than any conversational faux pas.

Is living in this time loop turning me into a sex fiend? Maybe I should slow it down, take it easy. I'm going to lose my mind from the lust. I need to focus on talking to Alex. Just talking. To learn more about him.

Things other than what he tastes like. The way his firm, lean, muscular form fits so perfectly with mine. The way he smells, especially the warm place where his shoulder meets his neck and smells like soap and man and sex.

My entire body flushes with heat.

Stop it, Jane.

"Golden Boy Pizza is around the corner. Have you been?" He motions down the street with a head tilt.

"No. Pizza sounds great." Anything to distract me from the never-ending thrum of desire burning under my skin.

Our steps synchronize as we head down the hill, passing restaurants emptying out, nightclubs filling up, dark laundromats, and a smattering of convenience stores. The storefronts are topped with second-story apartments, all of their Victorian-style bay windows casting creamy light down onto the street.

We hook a left on Green Street, and there it is.

The Golden Pizza Boy building is bright red, the name of the restaurant scrawled around the top in antique lettering. A giant neon sign in the shape of a hand hangs from the roof, pointing inside.

The bar is on one side, and on the opposite side a long countertop runs the length of the wall with a number of stools set close together.

I order a slice of pizza at the bar, settling on clam and garlic. Maybe if I smell bad, I won't jump Alex at every available opportunity. It's protection from my own dark impulses.

Alex insists on paying even though he just gets a water, and I take my food over to sit on one of the available stools. He grabs the free seat next to it and faces me, one elbow resting on the narrow counter next to us. It's cozy, squeezed in together with people all around us, our knees brushing with every movement.

Once I'm done stuffing in a few bites of delicious pizza, I enact the *talk to Alex and get to know more about him than his hands and mouth and body* plan.

"Tell me something about yourself," I say.

"What do you want to know?"

What do I want to know? I want the good and the bad. I already know most of his success stories, and I want more. I want the dark and twisty. I want it all. "What's something embarrassing you've done recently?"

"We aren't pulling any punches, are we?" But he laughs and rubs his hands together and watches me, his eyes crinkled at the corners. "Okay, I got it. Yesterday, I found out my neighbor's name is Jerry." He takes a sip of water.

"How is that embarrassing?"

"I've been calling him Ben for a year and a half."

I laugh. "Ben? How did you get it so wrong?"

"I think it was the ice cream. Ben and Jerry. I knew it was one of those." He grins and I can't help but chuckle in response. "Now your turn." He nods at me. "Most embarrassing thing you've done recently. Go."

I sigh. "I do something embarrassing every day."

"Oh really? Trying to one-up me?"

I nudge his knee with mine. "You've seen me in action."

"What, you mean talking in front of people? A lot of people are nervous about that. It's no big deal."

I shrug, heat crawling up my neck. We've talked about this before, but I've never shared this bit. I want to share it with Alex though, even though it's embarrassing. "People at work, they would, they would . . . they would make comments." I shovel in a big bite of pizza so I can focus on chewing.

It was more than comments. They would roll their eyes when I stood up to speak, or they would whisper to each other while I was speaking, or they would chat in the break room, loud enough that I could hear from my desk, about how they suffered secondhand embarrassment on my behalf every time I had to talk. Poor them.

His jaw tightens. "That's a reflection on them, not you."

I wave it off, uncomfortable and prickly. "It's no big deal." How did we start talking about me? This is supposed to be about Alex. "Enough about me. Give me more embarrassing stories. Don't hold back."

He laughs and I eat while he regales me with stories about tripping off the stage during a performance, barfing in the middle of his senior prom, and sitting in the wrong class his first day of college and not realizing it until it was half over.

See? This is why I want to climb him like a pole.

No, Jane. Garlic breath. Wait. Aren't clams an aphrodisiac? Or is that oysters?

After I finish eating, we walk back up the hill to the Saloon, hand in hand.

The darkness is softened by the lights of the street, nearby windows shining with illumination. Across the street from the Saloon, Alex stops and faces me.

His eyes are dark and intent in the streetlights. I know what this means.

I clear my throat. "Thanks for dinner."

"Thanks for coming to my show." He steps closer.

I gaze up at him.

He leans down.

"Wait!" I pull back, one hand pressed to his chest. His firm, defined chest that leads down to lean hips and a trim waist.

No, Jane. Bad Jane.

"We can't kiss. I have garlic breath." I cover my mouth with one hand.

He smiles. "I love garlic."

"Even garlic lovers don't want to make out with garlic eaters. It's one thing to have garlic on your pizza, it's another to taste it in someone else's mouth."

He chuckles, but then pulls me closer.

"Hey, pickle juice!" someone yells.

Alex turns his head and I follow his gaze. It's Leon, waving at us from the doorway of the Saloon.

"Pickle juice?" I ask out the side of my mouth.

"It's a term of endearment," says Alex.

"Really?"

"It comes from a drunken night when I suggested using pickle juice chasers for whiskey. It led to a naked incident involving lightsabers. Don't ask."

I face him. "I'm intrigued. You can't leave me hanging on naked lightsabers."

"It was just me and Leon, and . . . then my parents showed up."

A car honks and we both jerk in the direction of the sound.

"Hey!" Leon yells at the driver, arms flung up in the air. The driver must have been coming around the corner and nearly run into Leon crossing the street.

A second later, Leon is on the sidewalk next to us. He slings an arm around Alex's shoulders. "We got another gig booked next month."

Alex groans.

"Wait, wait, he was just about to tell me about naked lightsabers."

Leon's grin disappears, his exuberant countenance flipping to solemnity in the space of a second. "We do not speak of that night."

I glance between them. "But I *need* to know. Why naked lightsabers?"

Alex chuckles. "A more relevant question could be why *not* naked lightsabers?"

"I need to hear this story," I say.

"No story," Leon says. "We made a pact that night and it was written in blood." He presses a fist to his chest, gazing off into the distance, his expression somber.

Alex grins at him. "I think we actually tried to write it in urine on my parents' front lawn."

Leon nods, still solemn. "Right."

I burst out laughing.

"Tell me about this gig." Alex slaps him on the shoulder. "So I can try to get out of it."

Leon steps back, bouncing around and shaking off the serious demeanor. "C'mon, man, we're getting better. We're going to have our big break. I can feel it."

"He keeps saying that," Alex tells me.

"How long have you been performing together?" I ask.

They exchange a glance.

Alex sighs. "Ten long years," he says, the same way someone might describe a prison sentence.

I laugh. "Really?"

"Leon!" One of the leggy blondes is standing at the door of the Saloon.

Leon waves at her and then tosses me a cheeky grin, a dimple appearing in one cheek. He walks backward, arms extended. "My fan group awaits."

Alex shakes his head. "Our fan group is your sister. And her two friends."

Leon points at Alex. "Still better than none. Nice to meet you finally, Jane," he calls out before he turns and jogs back across the street.

I turn back to Alex. "He's funny."

"He's the best." He gives me a wry smile.

"How long have you been friends?"

"I've known Leon since second grade. We started the comedy-music thing in high school, just for fun. And no matter what I do, it just never ends."

I laugh, and he smiles in response, stepping closer

and weaving his fingers through mine, making my heart jump in my chest.

My smile drops and I swallow. "That's amazing. I-I don't have many friends."

Eloise was my best friend, but I haven't talked to her in months.

His brows dip and he steps closer. "I find that hard to believe. You're easy to talk to."

I look up at him, only inches away, his eyes dark and focused on my mouth. "I am?"

"Yeah." His head tilts.

I lean into him.

Then I remember. Garlic clam sauce.

I jerk away. "Sorry, I uh . . ."

He shoves his hands in his pockets. "Can I give you a ride home?"

This is new. Normally, we part ways and I take a cab. For some reason, not making out right away means I get a little more time with Alex. Note to self.

"Yes. That would be great."

Also next time, bring gum. Why did I want to not make out with him again? I can't even remember anymore.

His truck is parked up the block, a refurbished classic, the bright blue paint shining under the street lamps —a fancy vintage Ford Bronco. It has to be from the 1970s or something. He opens the passenger door for me, and I slide into the vinyl bench seat. The interior is spotless and looks completely new, but it's all analog displays. Nothing electronic in here.

"This is a great car." It feels like Alex. Lavish, sure, but at the same time unpretentious. He's not the Porsche or Lamborghini type.

"Thanks." He turns the key, engine rumbling to life. "It was my first major purchase after we went big time." He shoots me a grin before checking the mirrors and pulling onto the street.

"Did you buy anything else fun?"

"I bought my parents a house."

"Wow." I can't even fathom that kind of success.

Jane, you just don't fit.

I slap the voice away, focusing on directions to my apartment. There has to be a way to get him to come upstairs with me. I mean, that's why he's taking me, right? Isn't that what people do?

He pulls the Bronco up under a dull streetlight in front of my squat, two-story apartment building, leaving the engine idling.

My stomach flip-flops. I twist my hands in my lap to keep them from shaking. "At the risk of sounding presumptuous, do you want to come upstairs and have a drink? I have . . . water?" And toothpaste. I can brush my teeth and then we can make out on my couch. Or on the floor. Or in my bed. Or hell, right here, I'm not picky.

But what would happen if he did stay the night? Would he disappear in the morning? What if he is the key, the one to make time move forward, the love the psychic was talking about? I can't really say I'm *in love* with Alex right now, but I could see myself falling for him. Who wouldn't? I mean, look at him. I turn in the seat to eye him straight on.

He's smiling, eyes crinkled—and full of reluctant remorse. "I better not."

"Are you sure?"

He slides closer to me, tipping my chin up to meet my eyes. "This is too important."

I nod. "You're right." I guess.

"Can I take you out again? Tomorrow? This time I'll eat with you. And we can get something without garlic." His lopsided grin makes me melt all over.

I want to argue, to push him harder so he'll come upstairs and push me harder.

But he's too cute to argue with.

I laugh. "Sure. Tomorrow."

Tomorrow, and tomorrow, and tomorrow,
Creeps in this petty pace from day to day.

Sigh.

Can sexual frustration actually kill you?

Chapter Twelve

"Tell me about your parents."

Anyone else might be taken aback at rapid-fire personal questions on what is supposed to be a first date. Or pre-date. Whatever this is. But not Alex. He smiles.

Besides, we've known each other for months, at least, at work. If he thinks I'm being strange or forward, he doesn't say so. He's the epitome of easygoing. Even when he's being Mr. Big Shot CEO of his own company and giving orders, he's calm and steady and self-assured.

"There isn't much to tell." He grabs one of the fries from my basket and pops it into his mouth.

I cover my remaining food with a protective hand. "Hey, grabby hands, I thought you weren't hungry."

"I'm not." His fingers feint to one side, I move to

block him, but quick and nimble, he darts to the other side, snatching one from under my hand.

I laugh. "You're fast."

Tonight we came to WesBurger N' More, an old-timey diner on Mission with bright orange vinyl seats, excellent milkshakes, and a juke box playing Elvis in the back.

I made a point to avoid anything garlicky, and I even brought gum just in case. Maybe if I get him to drop me off again and then make out with him in his car, I can turn him on enough to convince him to come upstairs with me. It's worth a shot.

"Tell me about your parents. 'Not much to tell' is probably a good thing."

"It is. I have a lot to be grateful for." He rubs the back of his head and gives me a sheepish smile. "I sort of won the parent lottery. My parents are kind, support-ive, still together, totally in love. They married right out of high school, but they're also best friends, you know?"

"Sure." I don't know, but it sounds nice.

"When I was sick, they were great. Protective and loving. Basically, they're boring as hell. Tell me about your parents."

"Oh, um." I fiddle with the napkin in my lap, wiping my fingers on it. "Yeah, well, my parents are still together too, but I'm not sure if they're in love with each other or just find their partnership too efficient to change."

His head tilts, eyes considering. "That sounds . . . serious."

My laugh is brittle. "Serious is a good word to use. They're very serious. Very successful."

"What do they do?"

"My mom is a plasma physicist. She consults for NASA. My dad is a professor at Princeton."

He sits back. "Wow."

"Yeah. Wow." I manage to restrain my eye roll, but just barely. Not at Alex's reaction, but at the fact that my parents are genius-level smart and . . . "And I just got fired from my job as a junior marketer," I mutter.

"*Student* marketer." He leans in.

I laugh, this time with more warmth. "Yeah. My parents are geniuses and I can't even make it as an entry-level 'student.' " I cringe. Ugh. Why does he like me again?

He shrugs. "Maybe you were in the wrong field."

"Maybe." There is no field for me. I need the field where I can stay alone at home all day and avoid the rest of humanity. My field is introverted recluse. Anyone hiring?

"You told me about applying for work in theater when you first moved here. What about that?"

I shake my head. "That's not a career, it's a hobby."

"Says who? I was told playing games was a hobby and look at me now." He lifts his arms, as if showing off all of his scruffy glory.

"Yeah, you look like a million bucks. Is that a curry stain under your armpit?"

He laughs and drops his arms, putting his elbows on

the table. "It could be. So, your parents. They are basically geniuses."

I nod and grimace. "Even better, overachieving geniuses."

His eyes are warm on mine. Understanding. "That's a lot to live up to."

I snort. "Tell me about it. They expected everything from me and Eloise. Even as children, we were expected to behave like mini-adults. No mistakes allowed."

He frowns. "Mistakes are how you learn."

I nod. "Oh, don't worry, I made mistakes. I was an eternal disappointment."

"And Eloise is, who, your sister?"

"Yeah."

"I don't think you ever mentioned you had a sister." His head tilts. "Eloise. Eloise Stewart." His expression clears. A light bulb goes off over his head. "Wait, the actress?"

"Yep." I lean back a little, my hands moving to my lap to squeeze each other under the safety of the table. "My little sister."

"Wow. That's . . . cool?"

I wince.

He laughs. "I mean, I guess maybe not."

I look up from my lap and meet his curious gaze. "She's great. She's perfect. Smart, like our parents. She's taking a break from Hollywood right now to go to Stanford, did you know?"

"No. So she lives nearby then?"

"Yeah. In Palo Alto." I sigh. "She's brilliant and

gorgeous and meets every expectation, and I'm just . . . I'm just Jane." I put my napkin on my plate and take one last sip of water before we slide out of the booth to leave.

Which is really the brunt of the problem between Eloise and me. We've been growing apart ever since we came out west together. She moved to Hollywood and went big time and I went . . . nowhere. I try not to think about Eloise. I don't want to admit how much I miss her. She was my best friend our whole lives, but it's been a few years since I've felt like I could truly confide in her. Where did we go so wrong?

Alex follows me outside and we walk up the street, back toward the Saloon.

"You're not just Jane. You're smart and kind and beautiful. You don't need a degree or fame to be of value. We are not our accomplishments."

"Says the really accomplished guy who founded his own company and will probably be a billionaire by this time next year."

"Ha." He waves a hand. "That's what I've done, it's not who I am. It's not necessarily all yachts and parties and people fawning all over me all day long." He rubs his chin. "According to my parents, I work too hard. And unlike you, I don't have any siblings to distract them from my life."

"They're very involved?" My parents are overly involved. I mean, they were. It's strange that it's been months since I talked to them, at least for me. The last time I heard from them, I ignored Mom's call and she left a detailed message offering well-meaning "suggestions" for my meeting.

"Oh yeah. I'm sure they're still traumatized from when I was sick but," he shrugs, "they do their best to be present and not oppressive. They call me weekly and visit over the holidays, and I visit whenever I can. Most of their calls lately are demands for me to take time off work. Do something, anything, other than work. They bought me tickets for a tourist bus, one of those double-decker things. I still have them in the glove box of my car, where they've been for the past six months. They're going to expire if I don't use them soon."

I smile. Eloise and I did that tour when we first moved here. Before things got weird.

"Hey, Pickle Juice!"

We both turn in the direction of Leon's shout.

"I really need to hear that naked lightsaber story," I mutter.

The car honks at Leon, dividing Alex's attention between his friend and me, his brows furrowed.

"How did you know about the naked lightsabers?"

Oops. "Um, I think you mentioned it earlier."

His head shakes slowly, eyes narrowing on my lying liar face. "No, no, I'm sure I didn't."

"We got another gig booked next month." Saved by Leon, who slings an arm around Alex's shoulders.

Alex groans, temporarily distracted. "We might not survive till then since you don't know how to look both ways before crossing the road."

Leon waves it off. "People don't know how to drive."

"I might prefer death to another performance."

Leon rolls his eyes. "Stop being dramatic. Things will pick up, my man. You'll be there next month?" Leon points at me.

"Sure. Wouldn't miss it."

Leon grins.

"Leon!" Cue the blonde in the doorway of the Saloon.

Leon waves at her and then tosses me the dimpled grin. "My fan group awaits."

Alex shakes his head. "Our fan group is your sister. And her two friends."

Leon points at Alex. "Still better than none. Nice to meet you finally, Jane," he calls out as he jogs back across the street.

I turn back to Alex, hoping he has now forgotten about my naked lightsaber slipup.

"Can I give you a ride home?"

Phew.

"Yes. Please."

This time when he's idling in front of my building, I don't waste time.

"Thank you for the ride." I sway in his direction, my eyes glued to his lips.

"You're welcome." He takes the hint and inches closer to me and then his lips are on mine.

Even though it's not the first time, the magic is still there. Better than any magical closet. His fingers thread into my hair, angling my head. His tongue slides against mine. I groan, nipping at his bottom lip.

I slide closer on the bench seat, as close as I can get without crawling into his lap, although that is looking more and more like a viable option.

He breaks away. "Wow." He's breathing hard, air sawing in and out between us.

Heat fills me. I need him. "Do you want to come upstairs?"

His mouth pops open, but his eyes are hot and his gaze is heavy on mine. "I do."

My heart leaps. *Yes!*

His head shakes slowly, eyes on mine, hot and drowsy with need, and yet he shuts them with a heavy exhale. "But I shouldn't. This is too important." His thumb trails over my bottom lip. "Damn." He pulls back. "You should go. I'll call you tomorrow?"

I strangle back a groan of frustration. "Right. Tomorrow."

~

"WHAT ARE YOUR FAULTS? Do you have any?"

He lets out a bark of surprised laughter. "Are you interviewing me for a job?" He twists to meet my eyes as we walk down Columbus Avenue, in the direction of the Saloon, after eating dinner again. I'm starting to discover his likes and dislikes based on how often he steals my food from my plate. Maybe that's a flaw in and of itself, but I enjoy the intimacy of it.

"No, it's just that there's, like, nothing wrong with you. It's sort of disturbing. You have to tell me something bad."

"Let's see." He rubs his hands together. "I have terrible morning breath."

I huff. "That's not a flaw. Everyone has morning breath."

"I smell when I sweat."

I roll my eyes. "Let's move on from normal human functioning to the good stuff. And by good stuff, I mean bad stuff. Are you a loud chewer? Do you have a third nipple? Maybe an extra toe? Oh, I know, you're a compulsive liar and megalomaniac."

"You caught me." He stops, hand to his chest. "I'm a multiple-appendages-having egomaniac with an aversion for truth."

"Now see, you go and say stuff like that and I can't hold any of it against you."

He laughs and then taps my shoulder. "Okay. I've got one. A real one. I can get, uh," he winces and shoves his hands in his pockets, "a little obsessive sometimes."

"Uh-oh. Is this going to turn into one of those things where you follow me around, clone my cell to track all my calls, and lock my ex in a book vault?"

His grin is blinding. "Of course not. If I cloned your cell, I wouldn't need to follow you around."

We both laugh, and then he grabs my hand, twining my fingers with his.

My insides melt.

"I don't stalk people. But I do obsess over work. It started with games though, when I was a teenager, and then led to app design. Silly, mindless games were something to focus on other than my illness. I still fall back into obsessive patterns sometimes. Leon is forever pulling me from the brink. When I get really involved in a project, I don't take breaks. I don't sleep, I forget to eat. I missed a couple of gigs and Leon almost murdered me."

"I can understand. I mean, I get into a single-minded focus too." Like when all I cared about was getting my pitch just right. Or getting Alex to kiss me each night, to the exclusion of everything else. And now all I can think about is getting Alex naked.

How can I get him to come up to my apartment? Maybe I can lure him in with the promise of something other than my smokin' hot bod, because clearly, that's not enough of an enticement.

"Hey, Pickle Juice!"

This again.

Leon almost gets hit by the car, again. They banter, Leon is called away, and wait for it . . .

"Can I give you a ride home?"

"Yes."

After he parks in front of my apartment, he kisses me good night. Like every time, my body becomes liquid heat. Lust permeates the air and penetrates my bones. I get so worked up I might detonate out of existence.

"Please come upstairs?"

He rests his forehead against mine. Then he sighs. "No, I better not. This is too important." Sweet words. A light fingertip over my bottom lip. "I'll call you tomorrow?"

"Right, sure. Tomorrow." Can he hear my teeth grinding?

~

"DO you want to come back to my place for some coffee? Tea? Water?"

I'm trying a new tactic. Asking him over *before* we're sitting in front of my apartment. It's a long shot, but I don't know what else to do short of crying and yelling and begging, and none of that screams "sex me up."

We're walking up the street toward the Saloon. Again. I have little faith this will work. Alex cares too much about our future to risk it by moving too quickly. I know. I've heard it. Over and over and over.

But since my future doesn't exist, I'm not giving up. Not yet. Maybe if I ask at different points of the night, I'll get lucky—both literally and figuratively.

"Not tonight. Maybe another time."

Frustration is a volcano inside me about to blow the top right off my head. "What if we don't have another time?"

His hands are warm on my shoulders, his expression regretful. "What we have is too important. We don't need to rush things."

I groan. "You say that every time."

He straightens, blinking in confusion. "Every time?"

"Nothing, it's nothing." I pull away from his distracting hands.

"Jane. It's clearly something. Tell me."

"No. It's not. It's . . ."

I turn away, arms wrapped around my stomach. What if I tell him the truth? I haven't tried that yet. If I can get him to believe me, maybe then he'll, I don't know, at least stay the night.

My heart pounds, picking up speed as I consider the ramifications.

He'll probably think I'm lying at best. At worst, he'll think I've lost my grip on reality. But what if he's the key to getting the days to move on? To finding love?

I spin back to face him. "You're going to think I've lost my mind."

"Jane." His eyes search mine. "You're worrying me. What is going on?"

Before I can overthink it, I blurt the words out. "I'm reliving the same day. This day. Monday, June seventh. Over and over and over."

He stares at me for a few seconds. Then his brows dip in confusion. "What?" A bewildered laugh tumbles out of him.

"I know it sounds ridiculous, but it's true. I've lived through, oh gosh, I don't even know, a hundred of this same Monday."

He shoves one hand in a pocket, the other rubbing the back of his neck. "I, um, I don't know what to say."

"You don't have to say anything." I sigh. I'm

flushed, face on fire. Embarrassment envelops me in its sweaty embrace. "Look, I can prove it. Leon is going to come out of the bar in about ten seconds. He's going to call you Pickle Juice, then he's going to cross the street and nearly get hit by a car. He's going to tell you he booked another gig next month."

He's silent for a second, processing. "I don't think—"

"Hey, Pickle Juice!" Leon jogs out of the bar. The car honks.

He throws his arm around Alex's shoulders. "We got another gig booked next month."

Alex stares at him, mouth open. Then his eyes flash to mine.

I shrug.

Silence descends.

"What's going on?" Leon asks.

Alex coughs. "Nothing. Uh, are you . . . okay? Because of the," he gestures at the road, "car?"

Alex has never been this discombobulated. Did I break him?

He blinks rapidly, his eyes moving from Leon to the ground back to me. He frowns.

Yep. I broke him.

Leon waves it off. "People don't know how to drive."

Alex nods, distracted.

"Okay, well," Leon glances back and forth between us, from Alex's befuddled face to my sheepish one, his brows lifting. "I'll just leave you two alone. Nice to finally meet you, Jane."

"You too," I call as he jogs back across the road.

Alex faces me. He regards me in silence for a long moment.

I twist my hands together. My heart is beating so loud, it can probably be heard down the block.

Wait. I haven't felt this way in a long time.

Shock slips in as I wait for Alex's reaction. I haven't really been anxious in a long time. Not like before. How did I not notice?

I don't have time to linger on the realization because he starts talking.

"Okay. My rational mind doesn't think a time loop is possible, but I also can't figure out how you knew Leon was going to say all of that or how that car was going to come around the corner at that precise moment. I would think you were playing some kind of prank, with Leon's cooperation, because this is absolutely something he would set up, but I also know you don't know Leon and wouldn't have had the time to arrange it all so perfectly. So . . ."

I wait for the gears churning in his mind, analyzing every possible conclusion.

It takes a while. "If you're not sure, I have more," I offer.

His brows lift. Then he nods.

"You told me about naked lightsabers."

He releases a bark of surprised laughter.

"Okay, so no specific details, you were both very

close-lipped about it, but I know it was a thing. You've also told me about how you obsess over work because of your sickness. Leon has to force you to take breaks. Your parents gave you tour bus tickets, and they're about to expire." I blow out a breath. "You always steal my fries when we go to dinner. You're one of the most considerate people I know. And you're a really good kisser."

A smile flashes across his face.

I step toward him. He keeps his hands in his pockets, but he doesn't back away.

That's a good sign. Isn't it?

"Alex, I know it sounds totally bananas, but it's true. I'm not a stalker. I swear, I know all of this because you told me."

He is silent for a minute, eyes searching mine.

My nerves start jittering again. He's going to tell me to eff off, or take me to a hospital. But my nerves don't explode into panic, because I know if he does, it won't matter tomorrow. I hang on to that, the only truth I know. Tomorrow, I'll wake up in bed and he won't remember any of this. No matter how terrible this moment is right now, it's not forever.

What used to be a curse is now a lifeline.

Finally, he nods. "If you're going through this, then I believe you."

Relief makes me sag; I didn't realize how tense I was until he spoke. "You do?"

"Yes."

I swallow, breath whooshing out of me in a relieved

rush. "I really thought I would have to convince you more. Or you'd run away screaming. Or take me to the hospital for a CT scan. Which I've already done, by the way."

He chuckles a little. "I have to admit it sounds incredibly farfetched, and I would like to come up with a more logical reason you could know all of that. But I'd prefer to take you at your word."

"Really?"

"I try to believe what people tell me as they see it, not how I think they should." He shrugs. "That's where true understanding comes from."

Oh, Alex. It would be so easy to love him.

I squeeze my eyes shut, pressing my fingers to the middle of my forehead. "I wouldn't believe me." I spread my arms out before flopping them down to my sides. "The screwed-up part is that it doesn't matter. None of it matters. Tomorrow will be Monday, again, and you won't remember any of it. That's why . . . that's one of the reasons I want you to come back to my place with me. Or I can go to your place. Either way. I just, it's hard to understand, but I need to make something different."

His brow creases. "So you think if we spend the night together that will change something? Like having sex will get you out of this . . . time loop?"

"No." I wave a hand. "Of course not."

But even as the words trip out of my mouth, they come right back and slap me in the face. I'm lying. It's *exactly* what I think, and it wasn't until he spelled it out that I recognized I've been holding on to that hope.

But it's not true. Sex isn't going to solve anything, except maybe I won't be so damn horny for Alex all the time. My gut knows it, instinct telling me a truth I didn't want to accept.

His brows lift, waiting for me to pull myself together.

"Okay, yes. Maybe. I don't know. Maybe if you just stay with me until morning? No, you know," I wave a hand, "penetration involved?"

He laughs. "Have you tried staying up all night? On your own, or with anyone else?"

"I have, by myself. It doesn't work." I blow out a breath. "I've also tried sleeping in my closet. Nothing works. If I stay awake, I black out and it's not a fun feeling, and then I wake up on the seventh again. You're the . . . you're the first person I've told. Except a weird teenager and I didn't invite her over."

"In your closet?"

I shrug. "The closet is magic."

His brow furrows. "Uh . . ."

I'm making this worse.

I shake my head. "It's too much to explain. Just trust me, staying up doesn't work."

But another thought knocks me upside the head. What if Alex does stay the night and then he gets stuck in the loop with me? That's not fair to him. The truth is, I don't know what will happen either way, and I can't put this on someone else.

He can't save me. I have to save myself. It's always been about me.

"Hmm." He rubs his chin. "So it's likely that even if I do stay the night with you, you'll just black out and I'll end up back home like God hit a giant reset button."

I shrug. "Anything is possible at this point."

He nods, thoughtful.

I move closer. "The thing is, I like you. You like me. And for me, we've been dating and kissing a lot. This isn't the first night we talked and spent time together." I step into him. "It's not the first time I've figured out that you like it when I bite you a little, right here." I lean in. His hands lift to my shoulders, squeezing gently when I move closer and press my lips against the corner where his neck meets his shoulder.

He shivers. "Jane." My name is a breath hissed between his teeth.

I pull back, our eyes lock, and then we're kissing. And again, the fireworks erupt and I want nothing more than to crawl inside of him and live there forever.

Eventually he steps back far enough to meet my eyes.

I can predict what's coming next.

"I like you. I believe you. But Jane, I'm still not going home with you." He blows out a breath.

"I know."

I shouldn't have put that kind of pressure on him anyway. He can't make time move forward. Sleeping with him won't "fix" me. Am I using Alex in order to give myself a better sense of control?

Shame spreads through me, heating my cheeks.

Alex isn't the one who can give me happiness, like it's a gift to be obtained. I can't control him, and I shouldn't want to. If I ever get out of this blasted day and we go on a date or four, and actually sleep together, he could wake up months from now and decide he's not into me. If I put all responsibility for my happiness onto him, that's . . . ridiculous.

What did the psychic say? It has to come from inside.

Such an impossibility. But I have to try. Right?

I'm no better than Mark if I'm using Alex as my means of escape.

I need a break.

I take a deep breath and step back. "You mean a lot to me, Alex. Which is why I probably won't see you for a while."

He moves toward me. "Jane——"

"It's okay." I hold up a hand, letting my eyes trace over his features. "You won't notice. I've got to go."

So this is what it feels like.

To break my own heart.

Chapter Thirteen

"SPRINKLE ME."

I lie in bed, listening to the song that has become an intrinsic part of my existence and waiting for the moment . . . I point a finger in the air right as the neighbor pounds on Hugo's door.

I have the timing down to the second.

I mouth the words I know are being shouted outside, even though I can't hear them from here over the skull-splitting music.

I lie in bed, debating if I should go to work today. What's the point? I still get fired. I've tried everything I can think of and nothing works. For the past week or so, I haven't been leaving the apartment much at all, except to get food and see if the Druid Stone is open.

It's not.

It's not even there. The storefront, which I swear was between a dry cleaner and a Thai place two blocks down, has disappeared, like I imagined the whole thing. I've walked back and forth twelve times, and . . . nothing.

I need to do something other than lie here and mope and think about work and Alex and the fact that I haven't seen him in a week. Haven't made him laugh or felt his lips on mine.

My chest aches. I miss him.

The neighbor in the robe has given up by now and the music plays on.

Why does Hugo blast this song on this day?

Why does he cry every night?

I've never bothered to find out. The old me would stick my head in the sand and forget it, not get involved, not put myself out there, much less risk having to interact with a stranger and every mortifying possibility that comes along with it.

But once the question enters my mind, I can't get rid of it.

Why?

And it's not like I have anything better to do.

By the time I take a leisurely shower and get dressed in some jeans and a comfy tee, the music has stopped. Gathering the tattered remnants of my courage, I exit my apartment and walk down the hall to the neighbor's. I knock, a few short raps, and then twist my hands together. I'm a little jittery, but I can do this.

I've seen him around, so I know he's a big guy, but when the door swings open and he's actually standing in front of me with a questioning—*is it also menacing?*

—countenance, the reality is enough to make my throat close and my heart race.

Maybe I can't do this.

He's got to be at least six seven. His arms flex. Maybe a body builder or something. Hit man. Assassin.

"Can I help you?" His voice is a deep bass, his expression stone serious.

But the crying at night . . . there has to be more here than what it seems, and since there's no tomorrow, I guess self-preservation has been tossed out the window along with my sanity.

I take a breath and blurt it out. "Why do you play that song?"

His brows descend, a furrow forming between his eyes. "I know it was too loud. I'm sorry, I've had . . . a bad morning." The hard exterior dips slightly.

He's apologizing? No dying for me today, I guess.

"It's fine," I rush. "It's—I was curious and—" My gaze lands on a dress hanging just inside the door on a coat rack. "Oh wow, what a beautiful dress."

It's a vibrant red gown with a fitted top and tulle skirt. The tulle glitters under the light and I squint. Is there silvery thread embedded in the fabric? I'm itching to get a better look.

"Oh." He turns, glancing at the dress and then back at me.

"May I?"

He blinks, stares at me in silence for a couple seconds before stepping aside. "Um. Yes. Sure."

After a slight hesitation, I walk past him and pull it

down, further into the light, handling it with care. Thick tank straps connected to an A-line skirt fluffed with tulle, and yes, silver thread weaves flowery patterns into the fabric. It's clearly handmade and designed for someone of large stature. Someone the size of the man hulking behind me.

"Oh, no." My fingers graze over a spot on the side. I pull it closer to examine the seam. "There's a tear here." I glance up at him.

He stares at me in silence for a lengthy beat, and I think maybe he's going to kick me out or yell at me. This might be when the murder happens.

But then he bursts into tears.

Shocked, I stare while he blubbers with great heaving sobs, massive shoulders shuddering. What does one do in this situation? Is a hug appropriate?

I hang the dress back up and pat him awkwardly on the arm. "It's okay."

The shaking subsides, but the tears keep coming, tripping down his face.

Oh dear.

This is great, Jane. The first time you meet your neighbor after living next to him for however many years and you make him cry. Perfect.

"I can probably fix the dress for you," I say. "I'm pretty sure I have matching thread, or something close enough, anyway."

He doesn't respond at first, covering his face with his hands.

I glance around but can't find tissues or anything.

His apartment is set up like mine, so, leaving him in the entry, I run to the bathroom and grab some toilet paper. The counter is covered in jars of makeup, foundation, eye shadow, a whole box full of lipsticks of varying colors. He has more makeup than I've owned my entire life.

"Hugo, here." I hand him the toilet paper to wipe up his face.

After a few more hiccups, he gathers his breath. "How do you know my name?"

I freeze. Oh yeah. "Oh, the neighbor this morning. He was yelling it."

And it's hard to forget when I've heard it fourteen thousand times.

"Oh. That makes sense." He shifts. "The dress." He gestures to it with one giant, thrown-out hand. "It doesn't fit me. I was measured for it three months ago and I think," he blows out a heavy breath, "I've gained weight."

I look him up and down. He's literally all muscle. Weight where? "Oh. Hmm. May I?" I point at the dress and he nods.

I pull it down again, examining the seams and the tear.

"I can fix this and then let it out. Maybe an inch or two. Do you think that will be enough?" I lift my gaze to his.

Wide eyes meet mine. Hopeful eyes. Eyes sheened with moisture, but at least the sobbing has stopped.

I continue. "If we need more than a couple inches, I

could panel in more fabric. I don't have anything matching, but I might have a complementary color, and we could hide some of it under the tulle."

Hope and wonder fill his eyes. "You could do that?"

"Sure." I shrug. "I used to be a seamstress, just for fun. Before I started my real career." The phrase is rote, something I've said numerous times. I smile but it's strained. I suppose I should have said it *was* my real career. That turned out well, didn't it? I might have a roof over my head but does it matter if I'm living in purgatory?

"Who are you?" His voice is gravel, threaded with curiosity.

"I'm your neighbor." I stick out my hand. "Jane Stewart."

"Hugo Lamaire." He takes my hand and offers a courtly bow over my fingers that doesn't quite match his intimidating appearance.

I laugh. "Well, Hugo. Nice to meet you. Now let's see if we can get this fixed up."

"HOW LONG HAVE YOU BEEN PERFORMING?" I ask Hugo while I tug a needle through the delicate fabric.

"Five years. Harry got me into it." He points a spatula at me. "But we're not talking about Harry."

"No Harry. Got it."

I'm sitting at Hugo's kitchen table while he makes us

brunch, which is grilled cheese because it's all he knows how to make. Harry used to do all the cooking. But we're not talking about Harry.

"How long will it take to fix the dress?"

"Not much longer. When is the audition?"

"It starts at noon."

"Perfect." I give him my best reassuring smile, which might be more of a grimace. This situation is a little anxiety inducing, but I'm dealing. The only thing keeping me from shaking with nerves is the fact that I'm using my hands to fix his dress and sewing is all soothing, repetitive movements. Plus it's something to focus on other than my incessant monologue of worries. "This won't take more than another few minutes. I'm nearly done."

He brings over a plate with a grilled cheese and sets it next to me. "Did you want some coffee or—? Oh wait. I don't have any coffee. I stopped drinking it when Harry ran off with that barista from Oakland."

Hugo has a real gift for talking about something we're not talking about. "I'm sorry."

"Not as sorry as I am. Can you imagine? Breaking up a week before auditioning for a show at the Huntress? And now we have to perform together." He shakes his head. "If we win, we'll have to see each other even more. Rehearsals every night. During the show." He frowns. "Touching each other and pretending to enjoy it. I'm not sure what would be worse, getting a spot on the show, or not getting a call back and then getting a clean break, you know? Who wants to see their ex every day for months, right after he dumps you?"

"I get it." I finish the last stitch and then flip the garment around. "I think that should do it. Do you want to try it on?"

He swallows. "I'm a little nervous. The sound of the fabric tearing." He shudders. "It was traumatizing. Harry is meeting me at the venue and he will go ballistic if I show up with a torn dress."

"It sounds like you're better off without him."

He nods but his mouth curves down. "I suppose."

"Now you have a little more room, so it should be fine. And even if it does tear again, we have time to fix it."

I hold up the dress. After a second, he takes it from me, giant hands careful.

He disappears into the bedroom and I eat the grilled cheese, which is two slices of white bread with some fake American cheese, fried in butter. It's surprisingly delicious, and somehow comforting. It reminds me of childhood, even though my mother would have died before making a sandwich like this when I was a kid. If we had something as pedestrian as grilled cheese, it was on split wheat or focaccia with gouda and aged cheddar.

A few long minutes later, I've finished my sandwich and Hugo emerges from the bedroom. He's wearing the dress and grinning.

"It fits." He twirls around, sending the skirt flying.

I stand up and move closer to make sure the seam isn't visible. "It looks fantastic."

"You think so?" He grips the ends of the skirt and holds it out from his body, gazing down at himself. "I think blue looks so much better on me than red. Like a royal blue, you know? But Harry picked the colors and he didn't want us to clash." He drops the skirt and blinks rapidly.

"I'm sorry."

"Jane." He steps toward me, engulfing my hands in his. "Don't apologize. You're an angel sent to me straight from heaven. And I still have an hour until I have to be at the Huntress." He watches me, head tilted. "You should come with me."

Surprise jolts me backward, and I pull my hands from his. "You want me to go to your audition?"

He bites his lip, putting his hands together like he's praying to the seamstress gods. "Please."

Mingling with strangers is usually like asking me to swallow a live snake. My hands twist together. "I don't know."

"Pretty please?" His gaze is pleading. "What if it rips again while I'm there? I might need you. And it will be fun, I promise. And you can meet Harry and we can talk about how gross he is after."

Hugo is clearly terrified and anxious and scared. I know what it's like, to go somewhere and feel alone. I can't do that to him, especially not when I know that later, he's going to be crying like his whole world is over.

And let's face it, it's better than moping around my apartment or giving into the urge to see Alex.

I nod. "I can go."

His eyes light up, shimmering a little bit. He grips my hand briefly. "Thank you."

Chapter Fourteen

HUGO DRIVES US INTO THE CITY IN HIS CAR, A GEO Metro that's at least thirty years old. His frame fills up the entire driver's side and spills over into the passenger area, forcing me to lean against the window. There's a dent in the roof headliner where his head sits. The back is full, stuffed to the brim with all his makeup and hair supplies, the dress hanging from a hook in the back seat. The car rattles and chugs so much I don't think we'll make it across the Bay Bridge, but Hugo distracts me by telling me what to expect.

"The audition is for a new show with a 1980s theme. Harry and I picked this whole *Dirty Dancing* concept, because of the song 'The Time of My Life.' Even though the movie is set in the '60s, the song is *so* '80s. It was really Harry's idea." He blows out a breath and glances over one shoulder before switching lanes. "We have to show them the performance so they can pick the lineup for the official show. Everything depends on today."

"I'm sure you will be great."

He huffs. "If Harry even shows. I've been trying to reach him since yesterday, and he's not returning my calls." He frowns, tossing me a worried glance. "What if he doesn't show?"

I have no idea how to answer that question. "Um. Could someone else step in?"

"No. We practiced this for weeks. No one but the two of us know all the moves."

"Oh, right. Well, I'm sure he'll show. He wouldn't want to give up this opportunity either, right?"

"I really hope so."

We end up in the Mission District, where Hugo somehow manages to parallel park us between a VW bus and a Mercedes and I have to shut my eyes because I'm sure we won't fit and he's going to hit something, despite the amoeba-sized car we're in. But somehow, he makes it work.

I help him gather his supplies out of the tiny trunk and back seat, the makeup, wig box, and the dress.

I follow him down the street. We pass three vintage clothing stores and a vegan ice cream shop, and then I get distracted by a brick building splashed in vibrant art, a giant mural of swirling colors and faces of various ages and ethnicities, a sky- and mountainscape in the background.

"Jane, come on!" Hugo yells from down the block.

I race to catch up, following him into a back alley. He knocks on a rough metal door.

From there, we're led into the back stage of the venue, down a darkened quiet hallway and into the chaos of thirty-plus men putting on makeup and wigs.

Mirrors and lights line all four walls, and the middle of the room is pandemonium. Talking, laughter, half-dressed bodies, the air heavy with hair product and perfume.

Hugo points to a hook on the wall by a mirror and I hang up the dress up and turn back around. "I can wait outside?" I glance around at the chaos, the colorful dresses being tugged on, the elaborate makeup being applied, and then I look down at my jeans and T-shirt. I am so out of place.

He ignores my question. "Harry's not here." His eyes search the space. "But there's Queen Bee. Bee!" he shouts into the chaos, waving a hand in the air.

His phone rings and he turns to face me with wide eyes. "Maybe that's Harry." He picks it up and heads toward the door.

"Wait!"

But he escapes into the hall, leaving me alone. I stand there, invisible amid the chaos.

"Hey, where did Hugo run off to?" This must be Queen Bee, her torso encased in a gorgeous silvery bustier with fringe fluttering around her hips. A bouffant purple wig hangs down to her waist, complementing her dark honey skin and expressive brown eyes laced with purple shadow.

"He's taking a call."

"It better be Harry on the phone or I will whoop his bony ass." She shakes her head, the vibrant purple locks twitching with the motion and then sticks out one manicured hand. "I'm Queen Bee."

I shake it. "I'm Jane. I'm . . . I was helping Hugo with his dress. It had a tear and I sewed it and then he wanted me to come here and, um. I helped him carry stuff." I run out of reasons to be standing here in the dressing room with dozens of half-naked people.

Queen's perfectly manicured eyebrows lift. Then she laughs. "Girl, that was the perfect speech. You may as well have carried a watermelon. Does Hugo know you're stealing his part?"

My stomach drops. "Oh no, I'm not doing that, I could never—"

Hugo steps back into the room.

Bee lifts both of her arms into the air. "Speak of the devil and he shall appear. Was that Harry calling? Begging for you to come back to his no-good cheating ass?"

Hugo shakes his head, eyes sheening.

"He's a giant bag of dicks," Queen Bee says.

"Is that supposed to be an insult? A bag of dicks doesn't sound like a bad time," says another queen, this one with a cap on her head, wearing just a bra and panty hose and tugging a yellow dress over her head.

"Will you zip this?" she asks, giving me her back.

"Um. Yeah. Sure." I slide the zipper up for her.

"Have you heard from Harry?" Hugo asks Yellow Dress.

"Nope. Haven't seen him. Sorry, sweetie. He'll show, it's early yet. He's a twat but he wouldn't leave you hanging like this. Not even Harry. I'll string him up myself if he does. Who's your friend?"

"This is my neighbor Jane. She's a seamstress."

"Lovely to meet you. I'm Fifi LaRue."

"I love your dress." It hugs the lines of her body like a second skin. A closer look reveals delicate sequins sewn into the fabric, twinkling under the lights, making her shimmer.

How clever. The fabric must be something flexible to move with her body, and incorporating the sequins is going to look fantastic under the stage lights. It makes me want to run home and bust out my sewing kit and make something myself.

"Thanks, baby doll. I think I need some bigger chicken cutlets to make it work." She squeezes her chest.

I have no idea what she's talking about, but I nod along in agreement.

They chatter among themselves, and I listen in silence, my gaze moving around the room, scattering, unable to focus on any one thing because there is so much noise and activity, bright and inventive clothing, not to mention the makeup and vivid wigs.

After a minute, I do a quick self-check. I should be panicking. I'm in a room full of strangers, most of whom are half naked, but when I do an internal assessment, I'm . . . fine. Normal. Is this what other people feel like in strange situations all the time? Maybe it's because no one is paying attention to me. Plus the outfits and hum of activity are distracting, setting my mind buzzing over creating my own dresses, experimenting with colors and fabrics that will shimmer under the lights like Fifi's dress.

The door behind us pops open and a short man with thinning white hair sticks his head in. "Curtains up in ten minutes. The order hasn't changed. If you lost your list, it's up on the wall. Raven, you're up first."

The frenzied activity in the room amps up ten more notches. Hugo meets my eyes, his wide and panicked. Huh. Someone besides me is freaking out. This is new. Or maybe it's not and I'm just too focused on myself most of the time, and I don't notice other people.

"I don't think he's coming." Hugo's eyes are shining with tears just ready to drop.

Queen Bee rubs his back, her red nails flashing. "There are at least ten acts in front of you. There's still time."

He shakes his head. "You know how long he takes to put on eyelashes. *I'm* barely going to have time."

"Speaking of," Queen Bee pats him on the back, "you need to get ready."

"What's the point if he doesn't show?"

"He'll show," Fifi says. But she exchanges a glance with Queen Bee, and I'm not convinced either of them actually believes he'll be here in time.

I GO OUT to the theater's auditorium. Almost all of the red velvet seats are empty. There are only a couple other people watching on the other side of the auditorium, and three people down in the front sit at small tables covered in paperwork. The director or theater owner, or whoever they are.

Wall sconces keep the theater from total blackness, and the stage is aglow in lights, the wide space framed by a bright blue archway.

They call up the first performer. The lights dim.

And immediately, I'm riveted.

I glimpsed some of the costumes and makeup in the changing room, but when it's all together under the lights, it's a whole experience. The outfits are amazing, exaggerated, colorful, shimmering under the lights. Feathers, boas, dresses, sequins, wigs, everything. It's entertaining. Enthralling. I've never been to a drag show, despite living in San Francisco for the past five years.

The first few auditions are two group acts and a solo. Queen Bee auditions with other queens in a combination of diva songs. Bee is Tina Turner and with her is Cher, Whitney Houston, and Madonna. They perform an entertaining mashup of iconic '80s songs that has me clapping along—quietly, to avoid being noticed or interrupting.

A little while later, when there's a break in the auditions for the director and whoever to go to the bathroom, Queen Bee slides into the seat next to me, still in her bustier. "What do you think, baby?"

"It's amazing. Incredible. I don't even know how to describe it. You were wonderful. I don't think I could ever get up there and do something like that, it's so . . . brave."

"I would have said the same thing ten years ago, but it's easier than you think."

"I find that hard to believe."

It's like a whole new world I never knew existed. I mean, I knew there were drag shows. This is San Francisco. You can't go two blocks without bumping into a queen. I just never paid attention. I've been living my life surrounded in a tight bubble of mist thicker than Karl on his worst day.

On stage, an Asian queen with a poufy white wig and a huge wedding dress starts singing "Freedom!" by George Michael. As she sings, she dances, her movements fluid despite the abundant clothing, but as she moves, she strips, pulling off dress after dress, and wig after wig, each one a different character, a different person, a different life even. A suit jacket and skirt, a doctor in scrubs, a sexy body suit and then—nothing.

My mind is blown. Not only by the story it tells about the things we wear, but the design that went into each outfit. She must use Velcro tear-offs or something to make them all so easily removable.

By the end of the performance, the makeup gets wiped off along with the clothes and all that's left is naked skin, no wig, short clipped hair. He stands there, naked underneath everything. Well, not quite naked, wearing flesh-colored briefs, but alone, under the spotlight.

"Wow. I've never seen anything like it." The act of undressing, of wearing a variety of outfits, combined with the lyrics of the song tell a story I never would have considered. I've heard the song a thousand times but never really grasped the meaning behind the lyrics.

"Damn, that hunty did good," Fifi says from behind us.

I twist around. I didn't hear her sit down.

She wiggles her fingers at me and I wave back before turning around again.

"Are all of the acts lip-synching?" I ask Queen Bee while the stage is cleared for the next audition.

She pats my knee. "With drag, baby, artifice is the point. Lip-synching is a perfect representation of pretense."

"Pretense?"

"Drag is all about taking something mainstream and turning it into something uniquely queer. Drag itself is performance art, and a societal message. We're all born naked and the rest is drag."

My mouth pops open. "That's beautiful. And scarily accurate." It's like the clothes I wear to work, the ones my mother picked out for me. It wasn't me. It was who she wanted me to be. It was a façade.

Fifi snorts and leans in between us, putting a hand on the back of my chair. "Queen Bee didn't say that. She stole it from RuPaul."

"Don't give away all my secrets." She waves a hand in Fifi's face. "Whether you're a real queen or not, baby, you are a queen if you want to be. You make it yourself. The makeup and costumes, you choose that. And underneath it all, we're the same. And *I* said that." She twists in the chair to face Fifi, who just laughs.

We continue watching the auditions, songs, monologues and group skits, and my mind is abuzz with all of it, and with my own situation.

I've been trying to fit myself into a round hole when I'm actually a square peg. So I've been wearing down my own edges, making myself as small as possible to try and fit until there was almost nothing left.

Is that not a type of artifice, trying to be something or someone I'm not?

And then the universe shook me up.

After a few more acts, Queen Bee and Fifi leave to check on Hugo.

Ten minutes later, Hugo takes the seat she vacated. But it's not Hugo anymore. He's wearing a brassy blonde wig, the red dress, and fake eyelashes. I almost don't recognize him, but he smiles sadly at me and he's still over six feet tall and hard to mistake.

"Did Harry show up?" I ask.

She shakes her head. "No."

I wince. "I'm sorry, Hugo."

"Dolly."

"Oh, I'm so sorry. Dolly is your drag name?"

She nods. "Dolly Hardon. Bee named me. She's my drag mother. You like it?"

I laugh. "It's wonderful."

She smiles but then the smile wavers and falls and her head droops. "I can't cry because it will ruin my makeup."

"It really sucks he ruined this for you."

She laughs, the sound watery. "It's not him. It's me. He left because of me. It's my fault."

"It's not your fault. You can't blame yourself for other people and their bad behavior."

"All right people, the call-back list is up. If your name's not there, better luck next time, and if you're on the list, we'll see you tomorrow."

Dolly and I sit together as people crowd the back of the stage where they've put up the list of names. Laugher, whoops, tears, and loud conversation buzz through the auditorium as people find out whether they're coming back or not.

Queen Bee waves at us from the stage, holding her hand up to block the light and then shoots a thumbs-up in our direction.

"Looks like they made it," I say.

"I'm so," sniff, "happy for them." She dabs at her face with a tissue.

My brows lift.

"I am," she insists. "I'm a crier. I can't help it. I cry when I'm happy. I cry when I'm sad. I cry when I'm angry. I understand it's annoying. It was too much for Harry to deal with. Hence the barista."

"It's not annoying. And as for Harry, that's not an

excuse. If he couldn't deal, then he should have broken it off with you before the barista."

"That might be true." She nods and pats at her face again.

Queen Bee and Fifi want to go out for drinks to celebrate, and they attempt to cajole us to come out with them. But Dolly's not in the mood and I don't want to leave her alone, so we drive back to Emeryville together.

We go back to the apartment, mostly in silence, each consumed in our own thoughts.

We part ways and say goodnight. Dolly's eyes are sad.

Later that night, when I crawl into bed, once again the sobs leak through the wall.

There has to be something I can do. I can make this day better. If not for me, then for someone else.

Chapter Fifteen

I MAKE PLANS FOR HUGO.

Maybe I shouldn't bother. Maybe this is just me, doing what I do, avoiding my own problems and instead obsessing over something else, a futile attempt to regain control of the uncontrollable, but it's better than obsessing over Alex, or my dozens of failed attempts to keep my crappy day job.

Perhaps getting Hugo to stop crying won't make the date tick over to the eighth, but at least someone can end this day with joy, even if it's not me. So I go back to Hugo's and the new goal is to find a way to make Hugo happy. I have all the time in the world to figure this out, right? So I think and stew and plan and come up with something to help Dolly.

"What if Dolly had one of those, like, half-man, half-woman costumes? Then she could do both parts, right?" I ask Queen Bee when she comes out and sits next to me during the audition.

"I saw Glamamore do a performance like that once and it was fantastic. But baby, Dolly would need an appropriate costume and she's six seven. That means finding a seamstress three weeks ago. There's no way to craft one in ten minutes unless you've got some magic fingers."

No magic fingers, but I do have a magic closet. I stew on it until Hugo appears later and I throw the same question at him.

He shakes his head sadly. "It's too late for all that."

"What if you could go back in time and have the perfect outfit to perform the song alone? Would you consider it?"

"Of course I would. I know both parts, but there's no point. I would need an entire costume put together in my size, plus a custom-made wig. The makeup I could manage in a day, but the rest . . . forget it. It's impossible."

But it isn't.

And with that in mind, I get to work.

Day after day, I accompany Hugo to his show, even though I know what's going to happen and I can't stop it, at least not yet. I have to be there to offer some kind of moral support. I get to know the queens better. They are smart, crass, and beautiful, and they don't take themselves, or anyone else, too seriously. They really put it all out there, without fear. Or, as Bee tells me, with fear but also like a boss bitch who shows fear she can shove a size twelve stiletto up its ass.

I spend every waking moment I'm not with Hugo designing a costume and keeping it in the magic closet at night so all changes and alterations don't get lost to the universe.

It's half suit, half dress—the cut of the dress matches the red one, tulle and all, except I use royal blue fabric. He deserves to have the color he wants. I screw it up, over and over, messing up the measurements, needing to start over, but I figure it out and keep going. I have the time.

I find a long wig matching Dolly's current choice of tresses and cut it in half. I cut a top hat in half, and manage to piece them together myself to make the wig secure.

It's late one night when I hang up the dress on the back of the closet door and stare at it.

It's done.

It's ready. Tomorrow I can give him the outfit and he'll be able to audition by himself, no Harry needed.

A grin spreads across my cheeks. I can't wait! My heart thumps with excitement, considering his reaction. He's going to be so surprised. And excited. This is a chance for him to achieve his dreams and I get to be a part of it.

Except . . . I press a finger to my lips.

How do I give this to him without it being weird? How do I explain that I happened to have the perfect outfit, in his favorite color, and it just happens to fit on a day he needs something exactly like it?

I rub my head.

And what about afterward? I need to get the costume back at the end of the day to put back in the closet, otherwise it might disappear and I'd have to start all over again from scratch.

Maybe I'm overthinking it. Everything will be fine.

"JANE. You're an angel sent to me straight from heaven. And I have an hour until I have to be at the Huntress." He watches me, head tilted. "You should come with me."

"I'll come with you, but um, I should bring, I mean, I have something, uh, lying around. From a friend of mine. From before. Let me grab it. Maybe we'll get lucky and it will fit you. And that way if Harry doesn't show you have something, uh—"

"What are you talking about?"

"I'll be—wait here a minute, I'll be right back."

I grab the outfit from my closet and hold it up, eyeing it for the millionth time for any problems or imperfections. Maybe the seam up the middle could be straighter. I got the measurements from the current dress, but what if I did something wrong? What if it doesn't fit? What if he hates it?

I'm trembling with nervous anticipation, but not the freak-out kind, the I-hope-this-works kind.

I take a breath. If it doesn't work, I can just try again.

"Here. I have this." Back in Hugo's apartment, I hand over the costume and then step back, keeping my eyes on the ground.

I can't look. I twist my hands together, focusing on the clench of my fingers.

The room is pure silence.

After a few long seconds, I can't take it.

I look up.

His eyes are wide. He holds the hanger with one hand, his other running down the side of the dress, a nearly perfect match for the existing dress, but a lush royal blue. The male side is a simple collared black button-up shirt and black trousers.

He holds it up to himself, perplexed. "This might fit." His eyes meet mine. "You happened to have this lying around?"

"Uh. Yep. Try it on? See if it fits? I can make some minor alterations if needed." This was my big plan. No plan—a challenge for a person who uses lists and memorization and routine and control and order to just get by. But in this case, it seemed like a viable option.

Dazed and confused, he shakes his head. "Yeah, I'll try it on but, Jane. This is incredible." He squeezes my hand, his eyes watery. "Thank you." He passes me, escaping into the bedroom to try the outfit on.

It was really that easy?

I blow out a breath. No plan actually works sometimes. Who knew?

 ≈

WHEN THE MUSIC starts and the light hits Hugo, his male profile facing the auditorium, I'm a bundle of nerves and anticipation and happiness. We finally did it. Hugo is auditioning, without Harry the Jackass. The more he's told me about him, the more I want to scissor kick him in the shins.

Hugo sings the male part, his feet moving back and forth, hands lifted to a partner that isn't there. Then he does a kick ball change, flipping around to show the other side of his profile to the audience, the dark blue dress flipping and shimmering under the lights.

"Doing it solo makes the whole performance better," Bee whispers to me.

I glance over at her. "You think so?"

Her eyes gleam under the distant stage lights. "It's so much more honest."

"Honest?" I ask, eyes still on Hugo/Dolly, singing both parts alone, dancing by himself.

"Think about it. Listen to the words. It gives the whole song a deeper meaning. Makes you think more about what constitutes the time of your life. Do you, in fact, owe it to someone else?"

I nod slowly. "Other people can't make you happy." Something I've reminded myself of a lot over the past . . . many Mondays.

Bee shrugs. "Maybe they can, temporarily. I had a successful show one time. Long time ago—baby, we won't discuss when—but I've had fans. A lot of them.

Hundreds of people every night. Men telling me they loved me. It was heady at first, don't get me wrong, but after a while it made me realize people telling you they love you doesn't actually bring you any love. It has to come from in here." She pats her chest.

Fifi stage-whispers from behind us. "From boobies?"

Bee twists around. "No, hunty, from your heart." She scoffs and waves a hand at Fifi.

Once Dolly finishes and exits the stage, Bee and Fifi disappear into the back to join her.

I wait in the auditorium, eyeballing the people in charge of the show as they murmur to each other.

When they put the paper up, I hold my breath, waiting waiting waiting as the queens crowd the stage to read the list.

A few moments later, Bee's loud sing-song voice shrieks, "Con-*drag*-ulations!"

On stage, Fifi and Bee crowd around Dolly, a tangle of limbs hugging, squealing, and also grabbing each other's asses.

I laugh so hard I cry. I'm so happy I could scream. It worked. It actually worked! This day is different. Someone who had a bad day now has had a good day.

When I meet them by the stage, Dolly kisses both of my cheeks and then grabs at my hands. "We have to go celebrate. You in?" She beams with joy, her eyelashes wet with tears.

"Yes. Absolutely. I'm in."

∼

THREE HOURS and two martinis later, I'm regurgitating stories about my sordid past that were better left on the inside.

"He basically used me for sex and I was too stupid and naïve to realize it."

"You are not stupid." Bee smacks me on the arm, using the hand holding her martini, which sloshes over the rim and onto me. "This Mark person is the dumbass in your situation."

"Mark sounds like a Chad," Dolly agrees. She changed into the original red dress before we left the theater.

I frown into my glass. "Who's Chad?"

Bee waves a hand. "You know. Wears excessive amounts of cheap body spray, thinks only of himself, gives off a big 'I look cool in fedoras' energy."

I nod. "That's scarily accurate." I eyeball the fish swimming lazily around in the tank suspended above the weathered dark wood bar.

We're at Moby Dick's, a nautical-themed gay bar. We're sitting all in a row, me, Bee, Fifi, and Dolly.

"Mark isn't the problem. I'm the problem. I don't know what to do with my life and I keep trying to fit myself in places I don't belong."

And I miss Alex. When I allow myself to think about him.

Fifi rolls her eyes. "You're like what, twelve? You're a baby. You have all the time in the world."

I snort into my glass. "Yep. All the time in the world."

"Why is that funny?" Dolly asks.

"If I told you, you wouldn't believe me."

"Try us," Fifi encourages.

"Fine." What pops out of my mouth next can only be blamed on the martinis. And maybe the fact that I'm lonely. Even though I've been hanging out with Dolly and Bee and Fifi for a while now, living this Monday over and over is a solitary adventure. So I tell the truth, if only to feel less isolated for a brief moment. "I'm living the same day over and over again."

Bee pops a cherry in her mouth from her martini and chews slowly before pointing the stem at me. "Baby, that's my whole life."

"No, I mean literally. I'm reliving this same day over and over. Every day I wake up to that song, the sprinkle me one." I turn to Dolly. "Why do you do that anyway?"

Dolly purses bright red lips at me. "You just told us you're living the same day over and over and this is what you're concerned with? My musical choices?"

"I know it sounds delusional, but didn't you think it was weird I happened to have a half-man, half-woman costume lying around?"

Dolly shrugs. "This is San Francisco."

"True. But the fact that I had one that fits you?"

"That is implausible. However, this city has more drag queens per capita than any other part of the world. So not impossible." She shrugs.

I frown. "So you don't believe me?"

"I believe you, baby." Queen Bee puts a hand over

mine on the bar. "Even if we didn't, what does it matter? It's your truth and you shouldn't be afraid to share it."

"Thanks, Bee." I sigh. "So? Dolly, why the sprinkle me song?"

She shrugs. "When I'm upset the only thing that snaps me out of it is old school gangster rap."

"That's gangster rap?"

Dolly clucks with disappointment and taps the bar in front of me with a cherry fingernail. "There will be no bad-mouthing E-40. He's the founding member of the Click."

I shrug and sip on my drink. Maybe I should slow down a little. My brain is getting fuzzy. "I have no idea what you're talking about."

Fifi rolls her eyes. "What you need to do with all this free time is work on your Bay Area musical education."

Bee chimes in. "Baby, what you don't know could fill this bar."

I smile. "I know you're all going to forget this since tomorrow will be today, again, but I really love you ladies."

Dolly lifts her brows. "Honey, how much have you had to drink?"

"Not enough." I take another sip.

Fifi laughs. "So tell us what happens on this Monday every day. Is it as boring as it sounds?"

I tap a finger on the edge of the martini glass. "I always wake up late. On days I show up at work, I get fired. Then I get dumped by Mark. Or, I used to. But now I avoid him."

"Wait a minute," Queen Bee interrupts. "Why not confront him? You should read his ass. You could tear him a new one every day, and you're letting that opportunity go?"

Reading, Fifi patiently explains at my confused look, is what the queens call insulting, roasting, or throwing shame at someone. Then she lifts her glass. "The library is open."

"Yeah, no." I shake my head. "That's not really my style."

"You make your style. Listen to Queen Bee, baby, here's what you do. You get dressed up. Looking all tight will build confidence, and then you slam his ass. Just keep it short and sweet. Tell him he's so full of shit the toilet is jealous."

Dolly smacks the table with a palm. "Ask him, how many licks until I get to the interesting part of this conversation?"

Fifi reaches over and taps my arm. "But no actual licking. Don't forget to keep that tongue in your mouth."

"Maybe I'll try it tomorrow." I blow out a breath. "If I go to work. I haven't been going in lately." I smile at Dolly. "I'm glad the costume I made helped. I'll make sure you have it every day, even if I go into work, and even though you're going to forget all of this. Which is why I'll need it back when we get home so I can put it in the magic closet and you can use it again tomorrow."

They are staring at me, eyes wide, mouths open.

Dolly is the first to pull it together enough to speak. "Magic closet?"

"Yeah. I can put things in it and they don't get stuck in the loop." I wave a hand. "It's confusing, I know."

Bee interrupts. "Hold on hold on, let's back up here. What happens other than work, dealing with Chad, and helping Dolly here?"

"That's . . . generally it. I mean—"

"Baby, let me see if I am getting this straight. You have a lifetime to get this day right, and so far, you've worked at keeping a desk job, avoiding a creep—who you could avoid by just, I don't know, giving up the desk job—and the only marginally interesting thing you've done is make a costume for Dolly here?"

"Not entirely. There is a man," I admit, blowing out a breath. "A much better man than Mark, er, Chad, and it doesn't matter because it's doomed before it can begin."

"Who are we talking about now?" Dolly asks.

"This guy that I've liked for a long time. He likes me too, but we can never actually be together. Because tomorrow, I'll wake up and it will be Monday again and even if I get him to ask me out every day for eternity, then what? We'll have one date over and over and never move beyond that."

Fifi nods. "That describes most of my adult relationships." She pauses. "Except without the prude stuff.

Mine are just sex over and over. So really, it's nothing like your situation."

I laugh.

Bee rolls her eyes. "No wonder you're in a time loop. The universe is telling you to shake things up, honey."

"I have shaken things up. I have really put myself out there. But it still doesn't work out."

"I want to meet this lover boy." Bee slaps the table with a palm. "Where is he at?" She glances around, like he's hiding in the woodwork.

I shake my head. "Oh, no. No no no."

"Why not?" Dolly asks.

"I'm trying to stay away from him. I get too . . . involved. Obsessed. First, I was obsessed with keeping my job, and then I was obsessed with Alex, and now I'm obsessed with Dolly." I jerk my thumb in her direction.

Dolly puts a hand over mine, her eyes serious and regretful. "Honey, I'm gay."

I laugh. "I know, but . . ." I can't exactly say, you cry every night and I'm trying to help you. It's not my place, and I don't want to embarrass her.

"Bartender!" Bee yells. "Let's have another drink and go meet this magic man."

"I don't think—" They all whoop and cheer and order another round and I sigh.

Probably the worst decision I could make, but I miss Alex. I've been missing him. I want to see him. And I'm buzzed.

We take an Uber, and getting out of the car is a hassle because Dolly has decided the Uber driver is her new boyfriend. He finds it hilarious and even gives her his number.

We finally get her out of the car and the driver leaves, but before we make it to the door, Fifi spots a picture of Patrick Swayze taped to a pole on the corner.

"Oh my, Dolly. Look, it's a sign!" She points at the picture with one long manicured finger.

Dolly struts over, tripping only a little on her super high heels and then puts her hand on her head dramatically. "It is a sign."

"Oh, here we go," Bee mutters, walking over to join them.

Fifi and Dolly start fighting and bickering over who loves Patrick more, Bee shushes them, and I burst into giggles.

"Jane." I spin around at the sound of my name.

Alex is standing near the door of the Saloon, staring at me with wide eyes. "Jane? Is that . . . what are you doing here?"

"Alex! You invited me." A delicate burp slips through my lips.

Oops.

I cover my mouth with my hand.

A crease forms between his brows, one side of his mouth quirking up in a half smile. Dammit he's cute.

Oh, wait. I didn't go to work today, so he couldn't have invited me.

Dammit. This is why I don't drink.

"I didn't see you this morning. Presley said you didn't show for the meeting. What happened?"

"I'm not going back. I quit." I grin. "Now we can be together."

Okay. Really need to stop drinking.

"Are you . . . ?" He steps toward me, the confusion now turning into concern. "Are you drunk?"

"I loved Patrick Swayze. I really miss that guy." Dolly is hugging the pole with the picture of Patrick Swayze.

"I'm not, but they are." I point to the queens.

"Girl, you don't know who's been doing what to this thing." Bee is doing her best to yank Dolly away from the Patrick picture.

I snort out a laugh.

Oh, shit. I'm screwing this all up. "I'm sorry. This was a bad idea. We should go."

Fifi decides at that moment to come up beside me, lacing her arm with mine and fluttering her thick lashes at Alex. "Oh, honey, he's cute. You should definitely go full peanut butter for him. *Creamy* peanut butter."

"Hi." Alex sticks out his hand. "I'm Alex."

"This is Fifi," I tell him.

Fifi gives him her fingers and Alex shakes them.

"Dolly is the one over there humping the pole, and Queen Bee is trying to get her to stop. We should probably go." I tug Fifi with me toward the other queens.

"Wait, how did you know I would be here?"

"That's a very good question."

"She has a magic closet," Fifi tells him. "I wish I

had a magic closet at your age, because then coming out of it might have been a lot easier." She hoots out a laugh.

"Nurse!" Queen Bee yells. Dolly is on the ground, long legs straight up in the air.

Fifi runs over and pulls on Dolly's hands to yank her to her feet.

"Do you ladies need a ride home?" Alex asks, eyeing Bee and Dolly, who are now falling all over each other with laughter.

I nod. "That might be a good idea."

Alex somehow procures a cab for Fifi and Bee, who both live in Pacific Heights, and gets them sent off. Then Dolly and I get into the old Bronco, me in the front and Dolly in the back.

I must fall asleep on the way home, because when I return to awareness, it's still nighttime and I'm in my bed.

I sit up, blinking at my bedroom. The lamp is on. There's a cup of water next to me, a note with Alex's cell number on it, and Dolly's half-man, half-woman costume laid out on the chair in the corner.

Well that's great. I finally got him to come upstairs, but I slept through the whole thing.

A glance at the clock ~~shows the time~~. It's only eleven.

Through the walls, muffled sobbing.

My heart drops.

No. No no no no.

I don't know what to do. I sink deeper in the bed

and press my palms to my eyes. This shouldn't be happening. I fixed it. We fixed it. No one should be crying.

Dolly seemed okay, but apparently not.

Why? She's in the show, she nailed the audition . . . Why didn't that work?

Was it Harry not showing up, or something else?

There has to be a way to fix this. Whatever it is, I'm going to figure it out.

Chapter Sixteen

"Sprinkle me."

I roll over in bed. The note Alex left me is gone. Dammit, I should have put it in the magic closet as a keepsake or something.

Knock knock knock.

"Hugo! Come on, man, it can't be that bad."

Hugo.

The crying. He seemed okay last I remember. He was smiling, we were laughing. But what do I know, I was a giggly, drunken buffoon.

"It's Monday! I have a call in thirty minutes. Help me out here, huh?"

What would make this day better for Hugo? Maybe it was the booze. This time, I'll do a repeat but make it so we don't get so drunk. Alcohol makes everyone sloppy. It's a depressant. Maybe if he gets into the show but then doesn't get all drunk, he'll be happier and less likely to cry. It's worth a shot.

KEEPING a six foot seven glamazon queen sober when she's in a celebratory frame of mind is a lot harder than I thought it would be.

I get accused of being a Polly puritan pussy and manage to limit her to a couple drinks instead of twelve, but it doesn't help. We get home and she still cries loud enough to be heard through the apartment walls. So maybe it's not the booze.

I try other things. Maybe if we talk more about Harry, Hugo will feel better. Maybe he needs to get it out there, share it so it won't haunt him.

I even try to find the elusive Harry. Maybe if Hugo had some kind of closure it would help? Could I get Harry to at least show up and talk? Ugh. No, that won't work. He sounds like a terrible person and what if it makes everything worse? I wouldn't even know where to start anyway.

In addition to working on Hugo's mental state, I spend more and more of my days designing and stuffing projects into my magic closet.

Maybe I should go back to at least making an attempt to keep the job I have, to avoid, you know, homelessness and such. If the day moves on, I might be totally screwed out of a job and out of a good reference since I pulled a no-call no-show.

But the days don't move forward and I'm not going to worry about it. For now.

It's surprisingly easy to not worry about my job when I have dresses to work on, designs to mull over and try out. I experiment and try new things. I make Dolly dresses and I even manage to get measurements for Bee and Fifi so I can experiment with different fabrics, colors, and styles depending on height and body type.

The work never lasts. If they take it home, it disappears into the ether overnight never to be seen again, but I make some replicas of the good stuff they like and save them for . . . someday. It will happen eventually, right? It has to.

I forgot how much I enjoyed creating something beautiful from nothing, the rush of adrenaline when I finish a project, the hum of the sewing machine under my hands. Not to mention the joy on Fifi's face when I hand her the lush purple satin A-line dress, and the squeal and exuberant hug I get from Queen Bee when I show her the gold lamé ball gown.

"You should sell these things, baby."

"Oh no, I couldn't do that. It's just a hobby."

She holds the dress up, shaking it in my face. "This is not just a hobby. You are lying to yourself, but you can't lie to Queen Bee. Anyone would pay good money for this attention to detail. It's beautiful. Let them have it! The world deserves your gift."

I blush, but not in an oh-my-gosh-I'm-so-embarrassed normal way, in a oh-my-gosh-she-actually-likes-it-and-I-was-sure-it-was-terrible way.

Actually, the stuttering and racing heart and tunnel caving in around me have continued to get better. My anxiety hasn't totally disappeared, but the normal extreme symptoms lessen with each passing day. Is it because I'm distracted with a specific purpose each day, giving me something else to focus on? Or because I know none of it matters since the reset button gets hit every night? Some kind of combination of all these things?

I don't know, but it's got to be a good sign. *Right, universe?*

But the universe, that salty bitch, doesn't respond.

And the days don't move on. And every night, Hugo cries.

I try everything I can think of. I design a dozen beautiful dresses and wait to give them to him at the end of the night, when we get home. Something to make him happy before bed?

Doesn't work.

I get Dolly to open up a little bit about her depression one evening when we get back to the apartment. Maybe if she lets it out, if I can give her comfort before we part ways, she'll feel better, and there will be no late-night weeping.

So I go to her apartment with her, under the pretense of getting the costume back once she changes out of it, and then I tell her about my anxiety.

"My depression is a lot to deal with." She blows out

a breath. "She is a nasty bitch. Always showing up at the worst times. Making me cranky and antisocial, not letting me out of my bed. I cry over nothing. Literally nothing is wrong and it still feels like my world is ending."

I refill her glass of water and set it on the counter.

She takes a big drink and shakes her head. "Harry couldn't deal with it. But we're not talking about Harry."

"I really don't like that guy," I mutter.

"Join the club."

She seems better. Less heavy, like the conversation released something. So I have hope.

But she still cries.

Maybe I should go over there. See if I can help. Is that weird? Would it be helpful or intrusive? Maybe she wants to be alone, and I'd just be in the way, or I would say something stupid or do something dumb that would make her feel worse. How could I help? She barely knows me, even though I consider her my friend. She'd probably think it was awkward, some neighbor she barely knows coming over . . . to do what, exactly? How could I help?

I've tried everything I can think of and nothing works. Maybe this is one of those things I need to let go of.

And so she cries. Over and over and over again.

Chapter Seventeen

GOING BACK TO WORK IS LIKE PUTTING ON AN OLD coat. A coat that's been in the communal closet for three years, smells like moth balls, and probably isn't even mine but was left by someone else. But here I am.

I'm stuck. And not just in a time loop.

I don't know how to help Hugo. Nothing I've tried works, and I don't know what to do next. I need a break, to take a step back, and then the universe will show me some signs, or whatever. I'm not giving up on him, I'm just setting it aside for now. Hugo's tears, every night, after I've tried over and over to make him happy. It's . . . depressing.

Besides, maybe taking time off work has given me new perspective. And also, I really want to tell Mark off.

I'm different now. This time things will change.

"Jane, you just don't fit."

Sigh. This again. "Right. Thanks. I'll see myself out." I gather my papers and head for the door.

"Jane, wait," Stacey calls out as I'm crossing the threshold.

I turn around.

"That actually wasn't bad."

Blade clears his throat and she cuts him a look.

"If you find another job in marketing, if you keep putting that kind of effort and care into your ideas, you'll do just fine. It was a good idea."

"But not good enough to keep my job."

Stacey sighs and shakes her head.

Drew snorts.

"Thanks anyway." I push open the door and shut it behind me.

That was new, I guess. But I'm still fired.

Ugh. I lean against the wall, contemplating my next move. I need to go home and give Hugo the outfit.

I can't hear them talking in there. Maybe if I could listen while they discuss my situation, I could come up with a new plan to work through whatever they hate so much about me, but all is quiet. Something tells me they decided to fire me no matter what my pitch was. Of course they did. How did I not see it before?

I will probably keep getting fired, no matter what I do. I could have the most awesome idea in the whole known universe. It doesn't change the past four years. Every time I could have volunteered for a project but didn't because it meant talking in front of people. Every time I had to present an idea and stumbled and stuttered and screwed it up. Every time I shunned my coworkers. It's hard to work well with people when you do everything in your power to avoid speaking with them.

I'm so involved in my own thoughts, I forget about the next part of this day.

"Hey. Jane. Come with me." Mark grabs my hand, tugging me from against the wall.

I yank it away and step back. "Mark. Make like a tree and fuck off."

His mouth pops open. "What?"

I can't help but grin in response. And laugh. I can't believe I did it. Queen Bee was right. It's effective. And simple. No confrontation even, because he's too shocked to respond.

I walk away, leaving him alone in the hall, gaping after me. It's possible I sashay a little. I did it! I told someone off without barfing or running away! I'm changing. Maybe that means time will change. It has to mean something, right?

I move through the main area, but then I'm stopped by Presley. "How did it go?"

"Not so good."

"Oh no. Do you want to talk about it? We could take an early lunch."

I stop, eyeing her hopeful smile. She's always been nice to me. Every time I go into work, she asks me to lunch and I always say no.

"Actually, yes. I would like to. But I have to take care of something first. How about I meet you? Have you been to Saffron? I hear they have the best shawarma."

Her brows lift, surprised. And then she grins. "Yeah. I'll be there."

I head out the front doors, walking down the street toward the pay phone at the next corner.

Footsteps slap the pavement behind me. My heart rate increases.

Alex.

"Hey, Jane. You okay?"

I spin around, greedy eyes taking him in. The old T-shirt. The messy hair. The concerned eyes.

All I can think about is kissing him.

Which sounds sweet, but it's not a delicate feeling, it's hungry and visceral, a living thing inside of me.

"So, how did the meeting go?" he asks.

I open my mouth to speak. I want to tell him I was fired. Just so he'll invite me to his show and I'll have the opportunity to see him later.

More than anything I would love to forget the world by making out with Alex. But I can't.

"It was fine."

"Are you all right? Are you not feeling well, is that why you're leaving? You seem a little . . . distracted." He glances back at the building behind us. "You never take a day off."

I tilt my head at him. "Neither do you."

Maybe there's a way to spend time with him without the making out. Maybe I can convince him to take a break. He works too hard and maybe I can do something about it. But not now. I should think of something though. There has to be a way to have it all, take care of everyone and everything in one day.

But that day is not today.

I back up. "I've got to go."

"Do you need a ride somewhere?"

"No. I'm fine. Thanks though. Bye, Alex." I wave and turn and hustle up the street to the pay phone. It's cab time.

It's not easy to walk away, to pretend like there's nothing between us when I've memorized his scent, his lips, the feel of his body pressed against mine.

But I can't think of him now. That way lies madness and obsession.

Once home, I race upstairs, grab the costume from my closet, and then knock on Hugo's door.

He answers his door like he did the first day, all menacing and stern and I smother a laugh. The man is a grizzly bear on the outside and a teddy bear on the inside.

"Here. You're going to need this."

"Who are—?"

I shake the garment at him. "Don't ask questions, just take it. I'll be back later."

SAFFRON IS in the design district, squished between a Starbucks and a nail salon. The interior is all warm colors, reds and oranges. Booths in the front give way to an open seating area near the back. Red hanging tapestry curtains lend the area an exotic but comfortable ambiance.

"Hey." I find Presley sitting at a small booth near the front. And I'm only slightly sweaty and shaky as I slide into the seat across from her, and that's mostly from running back and forth across the bay.

"Hey." Presley hands me a menu with a smile. "I'm glad you came."

"I'm glad I came too."

She smiles and nods and I avert my eyes down to the list of entrees.

The restaurant is filled with the clink of silverware on plates, the soft chatter of other patrons. And between us: silence.

Oh no. We're going to sit here in silence the whole time, and Presley is going to think I'm a total loser and regret ever making an attempt to befriend me.

I shake the thought away. If I do anything stupid, I can always try again tomorrow. It's not like I haven't done that before. I take a breath and try not to think about it. Which means, it's all I can think about.

A sliver of nausea slips in through the cracks of my uber-cool, I-told-Mark-to-fuck-off façade.

What if it's awkward and strained the whole time? I didn't make a list of things to talk about. What if we have nothing in common?

I take a slow breath, inhaling in through my nose and then out through my mouth.

It's okay. Even if I totally screw this up, tomorrow I can try again. This is temporary.

My heart rate drops a notch.

That's better.

"So what made you say yes this time?"

I glance up from the menu. Presley is watching me with no idea of the mental gymnastics being performed inside my brain.

When I don't respond right away, she adds, "I mean, I've worked at Blue Wave for over a month and I've asked you to lunch or drinks or out to dinner with the rest of the team about every other day. Did I finally annoy you into agreeing?"

I smile. "I wasn't annoyed, I came because—" Wait. Why did I agree to come out this time when I've been avoiding everyone at work for basically the entire span of my career? It's a good question. I could tell her the truth, I'm stuck in a time loop in which I cannot change anything and now I'm throwing shit at the wall and hoping it sticks, but I decide to go for the simple and shocking. "I got fired."

Her mouth pops open. "You did? Are you serious?"

"Yep."

The waiter comes over and we order, deciding to share latkes and tabouleh with chicken kebabs and falafel.

"You sure we can eat this much?" I ask once the waiter disappears with our order.

"Absolutely. My stomach is an empty pit that needs

to be filled with Mediterranean food, wine, and my parents' approval."

I laugh. "Now there's a statement I can relate to."

Presley grins. "But we need to talk about you. What happened at work?"

My hands clench together in my lap, staring down at a scuff on the table. "Today's pitch didn't go so great." I mean, better than the last five million times, but not good enough.

"So they fired you?"

"Uh, well." I blow out a breath. "That and also I suck at my job."

She coughs, choking on her drink. "I'm sorry, I wasn't expecting, um—"

"Brutal honesty?"

She shrugs. "Self-awareness."

Ouch. "Right."

"You don't suck at your job," she rushes to explain. "You're fine at your job. I just think," she considers me for a moment, her nose wrinkling, "I don't think you like it. Maybe I'm wrong. But I'm not sure your heart is in it. You tell me, do you like working at Blue Wave?"

I don't have to think long to answer the question. "No. I don't like it." But how to fix that? It's not like I could get somewhere else to hire me in one day. And even if I could, it's not like I can start a career somewhere else. Not unless I get myself out of this day.

"I don't like it either," she says. "I recognized the job dissatisfaction because I feel it every day."

Surprise pushes me back in the seat. "You don't like working at Blue Wave?"

She shrugs. "It's fine. The job is fine. I'm not planning on staying. I just need money to live off while I'm building a following on Insta for my miniature collection."

My brows lift. "Miniature? Miniature what?"

"It sounds a little bizarre." She fiddles with her fork and her cheeks turn pink.

Is she nervous?

She bites her lip and then explains in a rush. "Basically, I recreate various buildings, different types of architecture, cottages, windmills, apartments, things like that, but scaled down. And then I post pictures of it. I know it sounds . . . odd, but it's a whole thing."

"No, it's amazing."

I'm struck silent for a moment, and thankfully the food shows up and I can think for a second while steaming platters of food are set before us.

There's this whole world happening all around me that I've been completely oblivious to. It's an odd realization, being no more than a side character, in the periphery, completely unaware of other people's realities.

We eat and I ask Presley questions about the world of miniature art and how she got started with it.

"Don't laugh, but I was fascinated with doll houses as a kid and it sort of turned into an obsession." But then she laughs, blushing further.

"I won't laugh. It's actually—it's really cool." I hold up a hand. "That sounds lame, but I mean it sincerely."

She grins at me, scooping some tabouleh onto her plate. "So what about you? What are you going to do now?"

"Actually, I have a hobby too. I'm not sure I could ever turn it into a career but—" And suddenly, I'm not nervous to tell her exactly what I want to do. Presley's willingness to be vulnerable and admit her passions has given me a strength I wasn't aware I needed.

"What is it?"

"I've been designing dresses for drag queens. So, I guess you could say it's fashion design." My face heats at the admission. I poke at my food with my fork. "I design and make dresses.

Her brows lift. "Are you serious?"

I nod.

"No shit, Jane. I never would have figured, you're always so . . ." Her eyes drift down to my sensible pink blouse.

"Drab?" I wave a hand. "It's fine. You can say it." I pluck at the offending garment. "My parents bought me these professional work clothes. I dress like this because it's expected. Or I thought it was. I do a lot of things that are expected." I get jobs I don't want. I sleep with men because everyone else does. I wear my clothes like a costume. It's my drag. But not the fun, colorful kind. It's literally dragging me down.

I should design myself new work clothes. Something with a lot of color. Maybe that's why Eloise is always wearing vibrant outfits, to be the antithesis of our staid parents.

She waves a hand. "Wear what you want. Look at Mark, he grows a beard and puts glitter in it for the holidays."

"Oh, speaking of Mark, I should probably warn you." I rub the cloth napkin between my fingers. "He mentioned to me that he might have a thing for you. I'm not sure if you're into him or not, but if you are, he's not the relationship type. If you're looking for no strings attached, then go for it. But otherwise . . ." I shrug.

She snorts. "Yeah, not surprising. The office Casanova won't be satisfied until he's boinked the entire staff. Hannah is still hung up on him. You know that's why she's a bitch to you, right? She was pissed when he cut her loose and started pursuing you. Jealousy is not a good look on her."

I snort. "It's not much to be jealous of. We were never a real thing. And it's over. He was a mistake." I shove a bite of falafel in my mouth.

"Did you know his wife died?"

I almost spit the food out on the table, stopping myself and swallowing before speaking, trying to reconcile those words with my knowledge of Mark. "Wait. Mark was married?" How is that possible? How did I not know this?

"He doesn't talk about it. They were young when they got married. Not even twenty, I think."

Once again, the world shifts beneath my feet. Just

when I thought nothing else about this day could surprise me, it goes and knees me right in the gut. "I had no idea."

"There's no reason you would. I only know it because we went to the same high school."

"You did?"

"Yeah, but he probably doesn't remember me. I wasn't very memorable. Besides, he was with Katie, and they only had eyes for each other. It was one of those stories, you know? Love at first sight, high school sweethearts, the whole thing."

"What happened to her?"

"She died. Some freak skiing accident in Tahoe. So sad, right? She was young, beautiful, and they were happy together, by all accounts anyway."

I lean back in the seat, food forgotten. "He's never said anything. I would never have known." And now I feel kind of bad for telling him to fuck off. Not that his wife dying makes it okay to lead women on to get them into bed, but still.

Presley shrugs. "I didn't know either of them well, but I did know Katie's little sister. And through the grapevine of people we went to school with, I know he hasn't been the same since she died. So, yeah, I know he's a total douche sometimes, but I think it's how he's coping. We all handle things differently. Maybe he'll get through it, maybe he'll be a ball sack forever, I don't know. I'm not excusing him, I'm just saying, it seems like he uses sex as an escape. So it's nothing you should feel bad about."

Mark was always desperate when we fooled around, like in a fever. Not with desire, but with the need to forget, even just for a few moments.

It's not really so different from some of the methods I use to cope with my anxiety, becoming hyperfocused on certain tasks, other people, avoiding things I know will trigger my anxiety. Or I used to, anyway. Except he's hurting people. Me, Hannah, who knows who else.

Have I hurt people?

My mind jumps to Eloise and my gut twists. Have I hurt Eloise? I couldn't have.

"You're right," I say. "If he wants to sleep around, that's fine, but he should be up front about his intentions. And with me, he wasn't."

She winces. "I'm sorry."

"Don't worry, I'm way over it."

After lunch, as we're leaving, she surprises me with a hug. "I'm glad you came today. We should do it again. I don't have many friends in the city."

"Yeah. We should."

I walk to the train station, regret slicing into me. I've missed out on friendship. All those times Presley invited me to hang out before, I could have had a real friend this whole time, but thinking I would screw it up somehow or do something stupid or embarrassing meant I had no chance at all.

Back home, I pick up the note from Eloise, shoved under the door, and read it again for the hundredth time.

. . .

YOU MUST BE AT WORK. I tried to call but your phone keeps going to voicemail. Call me?

-Eloise

THE MESSAGE IS INNOCUOUS ENOUGH, unless you know we haven't spoken in months. And not just months of Mondays.

I'm not sure I'm ready to face her. I don't want her to know what a failure I am. Why does she leave me a note without knocking? Does she want to make up? Does she miss me as much as I miss her?

Maybe it's time to bite this bullet. Soon. I'll talk to her soon.

Chapter Eighteen

"HEY, JANE. YOU OKAY?"

I turn on the sidewalk to face Alex, his lovely face setting off an explosion of warm fuzzies in my stomach.

He's clearly nervous. Now since I know everything that happens on this day, it's so obvious. I was always the most anxious one in the room and it made me blind to everything else.

As soon as he's within hearing distance, I decide to proposition him. "I'm playing hooky. Wanna come?"

His head tilts and one corner of his mouth ticks up in an adorably confused half smile. "What?"

"I'm going to explore the city. Want to come with me?"

He looks back at the building, then at me. "You're leaving?"

I was fired. Again. But now, I've really given up caring about it. Like for reals this time. I don't like this job. I don't know why I keep trying, except it feels like I have to.

I left Hugo the costume outside his door with a note this morning, and even though the fog is heavy and things haven't really changed for this day, I feel . . . better.

"Yeah. I'm leaving. I'm going to play tourist."

"You know, it's funny you mention that. My parents sent me tickets to the double-decker tour, and I haven't had a chance to use them. I think they expire next week."

I smile. "It's kismet. And I could use a break. Maybe you could too." I nudge him with an elbow.

He pauses, eyes searching for a moment before he grins. "Yeah. That sounds like fun. And on the way to get the tickets out of my glove box, you can explain to me why you're leaving work early on a day you had an important meeting."

I smile. "Tickets first."

He lifts both hands. "Okay, fair enough."

I follow him down the block to his Bronco and stop on the sidewalk, tilting my head back to gaze up at the heavy gray sky while I wait for him.

His head pops out from the passenger side of the truck. "Should we drive?"

"Let's walk. It's a beautiful day. There's a stop up at the civic center."

He shuts his door and jogs around the front to meet me on the sidewalk.

"Okay, first of all, you want to walk uphill?" He gestures in front of us. "Voluntarily?"

I laugh. "Sure. Exercise is good for you."

He shakes his head, but he walks with me when I stride up the sidewalk. "Second of all, Karl isn't pretty. Karl is an old gray-haired man with bushy whiskers who yells at kids to get off his lawn."

I squint up at the gray mist all around us. "I think that's actually an accurate description."

"So, tell me what happened. With the meeting."

"Oh. Yeah. I got fired." The words fall out without effort. Huh. I remember when that was difficult to admit. Many, many Mondays ago.

He stops walking. "What?"

I stop a few paces away, turn around to face him, and shrug. "It's fine." I'll be back tomorrow, anyway. If I want.

"You're really blasé about this." His eyes search mine and he takes a step closer. "Are you sure you're okay?"

I laugh. "I'm fine. Why wouldn't I be?"

His eyes narrow. "Did you stop by the edibles place on Mission and eat some gummies before work today? Is that why they fired you?"

I roll my eyes and grab his arm, tugging him along the sidewalk toward the bus stop, moving faster than the morning traffic lurching along the street next to us. "Am I really that different today?"

"Yes. Not that you're, you know, uptight or anything

normally. It's just, most of the time you seem sort of stressed."

I open my mouth to respond but he rushes to explain.

"Which makes sense, since I usually see you at work. Everyone is stressed at work. I mean, it's work." He shoves his hands into his pockets and tosses me a lopsided smile. The gesture is familiar. He always puts his hands in his pockets when he's nervous.

I blow out a breath. "I'm not offended. You're right. I'm normally a wound-up ball of tension. But I guess today I just decided to . . . let go for a minute. You know? Come on, there's a hop stop up here."

We stand at the curb, waiting for the red double-decker bus to appear. Tourists stream around us, a family of four waiting a few feet away, a tour group of elderly people lining up behind us.

"Have you done this before?" he asks.

"Once. With my sister."

It's a tour bus, but with tickets, you can hop off at any of the stops to look around and then get on the next bus that comes by.

He opens his mouth to ask something but stops when the bus pulls up to the curb.

We let the family and the elderly brigade go ahead of us, and then I take the narrow steps that lead to the top of the bus.

"The top? Are you sure? It's a little cold." But he follows me anyway.

"Oh c'mon, Karl can keep us warm with his bushy beard." I gesture to the air.

I pick a seat near the front and he plops down next to me, sitting close enough that our shoulders press together. The only other people brave enough to withstand the chill are an elderly couple from the tour group, but they sit near the middle, huddling with each other and giggling, holding hands.

It makes me grin.

Alex glances around and then hunches down, pressing closer to me. "This is not a warm beard, it's like a frozen cold beard."

"It's not that bad," I insist. Then the bus lurches into motion and the frigid wind whips around us. "Okay, maybe it is."

He laughs and, after a slight hesitation, wraps an arm around my shoulders. "We should share warmth."

"I'm not complaining." I snuggle in closer.

His brows lift in surprise, mouth popping open. "Um. Do you want to talk about what happened this morning?"

"Not really." I shrug. "Not because I'm upset or anything. I'm not."

"I can see that."

"I guess I'm not upset because I never really fit in there anyway."

"That's not true. You were great on my team. We worked so well together."

I hesitate, watching him. "We did, but then you had me moved from your team."

He blows out a breath. "Speaking of that, I wanted to talk to you about—"

"Alex, no. Let me save you some time. I know why you did it and I understand. It's fine. I get it. There was an imbalance of power and you were right to set me aside. It wasn't fair to either of us to start something if we worked together and with you being a client. You were protecting me. But after that . . ." I shake my head. "Well, so we're on the same page about everything, Mark and I were never together. He just said that because he's . . . he has some issues."

He stares, mouth agape.

I laugh at his dumbstruck expression. "Let's not talk about any of that now. Let's talk about something else." I've already had this conversation hundreds of times.

He shakes his head, still processing my avalanche of words and then he swallows. "What do you want to talk about?"

"Have you ever been fired from a job?"

He chuckles. "Actually, I have."

I widen my eyes. "Tell me everything."

"I was working in an ice cream store."

"What? Where was this? And when? I need details."

"I was in high school. It was my first job. I didn't show up one day and," he makes a slashing motion across his neck, "fired."

"Why did you miss work?"

"Um." He scratches his chin. "It's not something I share often, but I had some medical issues when I was a kid."

I take the opportunity to put my hand on his knee. I might be growing as a person, but I'm still human. And insanely attracted to Alex. "I'm sorry."

"I'm fine now. Wow your hand is cold. I can feel it through my jeans."

"Oh, sorry." I remove my hand.

"No. It's fine." He reaches for me, taking my fingers in his.

He has one arm around my shoulders and the other hand holding mine, our sides pressed together. I'm still cold, but I could stay here forever. Flutters fill my belly —proper butterflies this time, not crows or crabs or pterodactyls. I love being close to him. I inhale his scent: clean soap, detergent, and Alex. "I'm glad you're healthy now. But that still changes a person."

"It did. But I think for the better. And getting fired was good for me. You know how I feel about failure."

The bus stops and some people down below exit and more passengers get on. A trio of teenagers braves the top, sitting behind the elderly couple.

I grin at Alex. "You love failure. You want to marry it."

He nods. "Failure is awesome."

I laugh. "Right. So you've said."

"It is. My failures are a part of me. They are me." He shrugs. "Besides, I've always learned more from failure than from success. Success isn't always all it's cracked up to be."

"Oh yeah, Mr. Millionaire? Tell me how hard it is while you're crying into your crisp fifty-dollar bills."

He laughs. "It's true. Success can be worse than failure in some ways."

"That does not feel accurate."

"When we launched our first app and had initial success, I really thought I had made it. But then it stopped selling and my next three ideas were complete flops. The failures forced me to step back and take a harder look at things, something I wouldn't have done if they had all done well. Success can be scary. Once you have notoriety, you have critics. You have something to live up to. Failure can force you to learn. There's a certain measure of freedom when you're a nobody and no one else is watching."

"That's true." I'm free. No job, no responsibilities. Not really. I tilt my head back as the bus starts up again, the wind whipping my hair around my face.

"Are you really okay with what happened this morning?"

I shrug. "It's fine." And it won't matter tomorrow. "I didn't fit in there anyway. I have a hard time talking to people." And I'm always terrified. Scared of rejection, scared my parents are right and I'm nothing but mediocre and everyone can tell. Alex loves his failures because they're a part of him. I hate my failures . . . for the same reason?

I don't have time to contemplate that line of thought.

"You seem like you're doing fine with me."

I smile. "That's different." The bus stops and I

glance around. We're in the shopping district on Fillmore. "Are you hungry?"

He smiles. "I could eat. And I know exactly where we should go."

"TA DA!" He holds two hands up to the sign above the sidewalk, a black painted metal placard that has letters cut out in all caps. *Jane*, it reads.

I laugh. "Perfect."

We eat sandwiches. I get turkey with brie and Alex gets a club with avocado aioli and we split them, each taking half.

"You love stealing my food, even when you aren't hungry."

His expression turns quizzical. "How did you know that about me? I'm a terrible food thief. It's not one of my finer qualities."

I shrug. "Must be intuition."

After lunch, we walk up Fillmore, passing seafood restaurants and peering in the windows of upscale boutiques with displays of headless white mannequins in sleek European styles. The street is lined with trees, the breeze tickling the leaves above us. I shiver and Alex steps closer. We have to stop at one point when we find a bathroom because I've been holding it for three blocks.

When I emerge a few moments later, I think I've lost Alex, because he's not among the random people meandering the Fillmore ~~early~~ on a Monday morning. I start walking back toward the bus stop to see if he's waiting there, but then halt in my tracks.

He's walking out of Athleta.

"Here." He hands me a black zip-up hoodie that probably cost more than my psychic reading. "For the ride back. So we don't get chilly."

"You didn't have to," I say, but I take the garment anyway. He bought me a sweater. I was cold and he bought me a sweater. I guess I shouldn't have expected any less from Alex.

His smile is lopsided. "I wanted to."

I meet his eyes. "Thank you."

His smile grows. "Shall we?" he asks, motioning toward the bus stop.

We stay on the bus all the way over the Golden Gate Bridge, the air colder and more aggressive than it was within the city. I lean my head back, gazing up at the burnished red arches, the fog threading its way through the cables, the tower disappearing into the mist above us. We sail underneath the monolithic structure and Alex leans his head next to mine.

On the other side, the bus veers off the main road and eventually stops to turn around at Vista Point.

We have about twenty minutes to look around before the bus leaves again, so we get off to stretch our legs.

"You said you've done this before? With your sister? When was that?" he asks. We're leaning against a rock wall facing the Golden Gate Bridge. Tourists roam around us taking pictures of the bridge and the bay and the cloud-covered vista.

I stare out over the choppy, slate-colored water, the waves a reflection of the ashen sky, the wind biting my cheeks. "It was when we first moved out here from Virginia. It was like, oh, five years ago now. So it's been a while."

"Does she still live here? You've never talked about her."

I hesitate. Alex and I have had this conversation before, but of course, he doesn't remember. "My sister is Eloise Stewart."

"Eloise Stewart." His expression clears. "Wait, the actress?"

"Yep." I sigh. "She lives in Palo Alto right now. She's taking a break from acting to go to Stanford." I blow out a breath, looking up into the fog and hugging the new sweater around me like a shield. "We haven't talked in a while. I've been avoiding her. Like I do with most things that make me uncomfortable, not realizing avoiding it makes it worse." I shake my head. "But that's not entirely true. I do know I need to confront the issue, I just choose not to because I think staying in a little bubble will keep me safe."

He watches me as I talk, listening intently, considering my words, doing that Alex thing of rolling with my thoughts no matter how strange or random they seem.

"That's the thing with bubbles. They're easy to pop."

"Ain't that the truth."

Eloise and I fought, months ago, because she told me the truth and I became defensive. She saw that I was miserable, and she was trying to help me, but I wasn't ready to hear it. So I yelled at her. And she left. And we haven't spoken since. "I'm going to talk to her though. Soon. I need to just do it. I'm going to do it."

This invisible wall between Eloise and me is one of my own making. Eloise can't help who she is any more than I can make time move forward.

And still, I've been holding it against her.

His hand reaches over, covering my hand. "You will. You always impress me with your ability to do things even if you're scared of them."

I smile. He's told me this already.

And he's not wrong, exactly. There have been plenty of times in the past I've wanted to run away and avoid everything and yet I didn't. But only with the little things. The easier things. Presenting at work when there's no other choice, forcing myself to make small talk with acquaintances I can't otherwise avoid, over-coming fear of a crowded train. But when it comes to the larger, more important confrontations, I still do everything in my power to run away. I haven't spoken with Eloise or my parents, and I'm still evading the truth about myself. I'm not brave. Not really. Not as Alex sees me. I wish I were.

My heart wrenches in my chest, the organ pressing relentlessly at my breast bone.

"You aren't nervous around me, are you?" He tosses me a sly grin.

Well, we have spent basically months together and I know what your lips feel like and I've memorized the gold flecks in your eyes and the feel of your hands. But I can't tell him that.

"I've always liked you, Alex."

His smile spreads across his face, and the heat of it melts my insides as if he's the sun shining through the fog. "Hey listen, I'm in a band. We have a gig tonight. I mean, it's not a big thing, we're the opening act and it's at the Saloon, but you should come." He straightens and his expression clouds. "Wait. Is this weird? Since we've spent most of the day together already, I don't want to make it weird."

I smile. "It's not weird. I had fun today."

I want to spend every day with him. Every night. I want to share all the bits and pieces of myself, good, bad, indifferent. It doesn't matter. He sees the best possible version of me.

What a notion, to be understood and accepted, exactly as I am.

And then the ground drops out from under me.

Holy shit.

I love him.

Chapter Nineteen

I SHOULD HAVE SEEN THIS COMING. I'M IN LOVE WITH Alex. This isn't a crush. This isn't my normal, anxiety-prone obsession. This isn't lust. I mean, it's not *only* lust.

I love him.

This should be an overwhelming discovery. A breathtaking adventure. A remarkable revelation. But it's not.

The psychic child told me I could get through with love. Well, here I am in love, but it's not getting me to the next day.

Frustration is my constant companion. It itches at me, pokes me in the sides, stabs me in the heart. It never stops.

Time passes, and I'm still in love, and I'm still stuck on Monday, June seventh.

Love is not all rainbows and flowers and unicorns.

It's agonizing. Hellish. Horrific.

I love someone and can never be with him. Not really. There is no happily ever after. There isn't even a tomorrow.

My heart, the blasted overreacting organ, it's broken. Hurting. My chest aches. How is this even a thing?

Grasping for something, anything positive about this situation, I make a list.

Maybe I should just be happy he likes me. Great. He'll never move beyond like.

I can get to know him a little better every day, but I can't have those future moments, the little quirks and foibles that only come out when you've known someone forever and are truly comfortable because they know you too.

I want to know if he squeezes the toothpaste from the bottom. I want to know if he's cranky when he's sick. I want to do boring things with him, like sit on the couch after a long day and watch movies. I want our own secret language, a lexicon of words and gestures that only we understand. I want to have entire conversation with a single look—one that isn't one-sided because I'm the only one who knows we've discussed something before a hundred times.

With Alex, I can have an endless string of these same twenty-four hours, but it's not enough. It's a slog every time to get to the ever-briefer moments of new, shiny stuff. I want it *all* to be brand new. I want all the hours. I want all the days. I want a future, the highs and lows and everything in between.

Maybe I'm selfish.

How many people out there would love an endless day with their person?

But even trying to hold on to gratitude doesn't stop the hurt. He will never love me back. He can't.

He won't ever have the time to get to know me and fall in love with me. I have all this time with him, but for him, it's just one day.

This is the worst unrequited love ever, because even if he likes me a lot, there's no path forward.

My natural proclivity for avoidance returns with a fiery hot vengeance. If I stay isolated, I can't be hurt. But I'm already hurt, so that doesn't even make sense. More hurt. I can't be more hurt.

I leave the apartment each day only to give Hugo his outfit—I can't totally let him down. Even if it doesn't fix everything, I'm not a monster.

I also try to find the Druid's Stone, again, so I can tell the teenage psychic she's wrong. I'm in love and I'm still here and she's full of shit. But I don't get the satisfaction because it's still gone. It's like it never existed. I even ask the lady working in the Thai food place next door, but she shakes her head and smiles and feeds me curry puffs.

I'm home every day at 3:07 when Eloise sticks the note under the door. Every day, when she doesn't bother to knock and just slips me a note.

Alex said I was brave, and yet I'm still not facing the music with Eloise. Or anyone or anything else right now.

Was he wrong about me? Maybe he only thinks he likes me, or he likes some false version of me, and if the days move forward and he discovers what a true coward I am, his feelings will change.

I can't have that. I will face this final hurdle, but not for Alex. For me.

Eloise was . . . *is* my closest friend. Even though we are nothing alike, and we fight sometimes, we've always had each other's backs.

Until we didn't.

We moved to the West Coast together five years ago. We lived together, shared an apartment. But then Eloise was going to LA all the time for auditions and eventually moved down there. Then she got her big break, a starring role in a Netflix dramedy.

Everything changed. She stopped calling. Stopped texting. Our conversations went from daily to weekly to once a month. But I just wrote it off. She was busy. Too busy for me, and I got it. I was fine with it, or I thought I was. I had other things to worry about too. And she would come up and visit during breaks in production and regale me with all kinds of funny stories. She was so happy. So successful.

I wasn't. But I pretended I was.

Then she called me on it.

"Are you sure you're happy here?" she asked the last time we spoke. We were in my apartment, eating Chinese takeout and watching *Grey's Anatomy*.

I grabbed the last crab rangoon from the box. "Of course I am. Why wouldn't I be?"

Her tone was soft, but her gaze was pitying. "I don't know. The job at Blue Wave sounds fine, it just doesn't seem like . . . you."

"Why not? What's wrong with me?" Defensiveness sent the pitch of my voice three octaves higher.

Eloise's voice was calm. Sensible. "There's nothing wrong with you. That's not what I'm saying."

Her self-assuredness in the face of my own self-doubt was like a lance to the gut. So naturally, I lashed out. "What about you?"

She blinked rapidly. "What about me?"

I put my chopsticks and takeout container back on the coffee table. "You have no idea what's going on in my life. You never return my calls. I feel like a celebrity stalker or something."

"I know, and I'm sorry. It's so busy in LA. Work is insane."

My jaw clenched. This is always her excuse. Too busy, too important, too famous for her poor older sister, the loser. "You say you don't have time to call, but I know you have time to brunch with friends at the Ivy."

"Jane, I've invited you down to visit so many times." She leaned forward, eyes earnest. "You can come anytime and stay with me and meet my friends. But you don't. You always have excuses. I'm the one who always comes up here to visit, never the other way around. It's a two-way street."

I shook my head. "You know why I don't come."

Her hands flipped into the air. "You can't let anxiety turn you into a hermit. I can't be your only person. You need more people and to put herself out there. It's scary but it's worth it."

I stood, picking up the empty food cartons to throw in the trash, walking away from her. "You don't understand. It's easy for you."

"You don't even try!" she yelled at my back.

I spun around. "You know what, I get enough criticism from Mom. I don't need it from you too. You're just like her."

When the words flew out of my mouth, I wished I could snatch them back and swallow them. But it was too late. It was already out there. I'd compared her to Mom. Probably the biggest insult I could have flung at her.

She stared, her mouth gaping open. It took her a minute to speak. Maybe she was waiting for me to take it back, to apologize. I should have. But I didn't.

"Maybe I should leave," she finally said.

"Maybe you should."

I should have apologized, but I was ashamed. She was right to be angry.

But now, she's back and she's trying and it's time for me to try too.

And I know exactly when to catch her in the act.

It's time to come clean. Put it behind us. I miss my sister. She's basically my only friend and I totally shoved her out of my life.

I swing open the door right as she's digging in her purse, probably for a pen and paper. "Eloise."

"You're home." Her perfectly manicured brows lift

in surprise. She's wearing dark orange, wide-leg pants, a top that's cinched at the waist and a cute little denim jacket. It looks perfect on her, but would make me look like an Oompa-Loompa. After a pause, she steps into me, enveloping me in a hug that smells like vanilla and sunshine and home.

A wave of nostalgia crashes over me.

We used to be close, a united force against the stalwart force of our mother. A team.

She steps back. "I thought you'd be at work."

So that's why she's coming over in the middle of the day and not bothering to knock. To leave me a note when she knows I'm not home.

But why bother?

I clasp my hands in front of me. I need to ask. To push through this.

I can't control anything she feels, says, or does, but I can control my part in our relationship.

"Do you want some tea or something?"

She nods. "Yes. Please."

I move into the kitchen. She shuts the door behind her, clutching a small vintage purse in her hands.

I turn on the electric kettle on the counter and grab some mugs and tea bags from the cupboard.

Eloise stands in the doorway between the kitchen and the living room, her eyes following me.

"Darjeeling okay?" I ask over my shoulder.

"Yes. Thank you."

"You can sit down."

She nods, blonde head jerking up and down, and then disappears into the living room.

The kettle heats. I bring the cups over to where she's perched on the corner of my couch like she's scared to relax.

I sit next to her. "I'm glad you came over."

She turns, angling her body in my direction. "You are?"

And then I tell her something I should have said a long time ago. "I need to apologize."

She blinks. "You do?"

"I know we haven't been close in a long time, and it's mostly my fault." My voice is only slightly tremulous as I speak. But it's not with worry. It's with relief.

Her mouth pops open.

I continue. The only way out is through. "The truth is that I've been jealous."

She makes a strangled sound, coughing, and then puts her mug on the coffee table. She takes a breath and then meets my gaze. "Jane, you have no reason to be jealous of me. And I'm the one that should be apologizing. I was pushy and overbearing, I was . . . Mom." She grimaces. "I've spent my whole life trying to not be our mom."

I laugh. "Me too. You aren't Mom. And you were right, but I wasn't ready to hear it."

She shakes her head. "No. I wasn't right. You can do whatever you want. It's not my place to tell you how to live your life."

I put my mug down next to hers. "You didn't. You

want me to be happy and I wasn't. But I wasn't in the right place to hear it. It has nothing to do with you and everything to do with my own weaknesses."

"Jane, you're not—"

I hold up a stalling hand. "It's okay. I could never measure up to you. Mom is always comparing my accomplishments to yours." I wince. "Such as they are. You've always been the outgoing and vivacious one. I was the shy loner. And that's not your fault. I thought I could be impressive. I tried to fit myself into a round hole, but I'm a square peg." I shake my head. "No, it's worse. I'm an octagon. Or a rhombus."

She laughs but then taps me on the arm. "There's nothing wrong with being a rhombus. I'm the one who should apologize. You were right. I wasn't making time for you. I was avoiding you first, and it's because I was ashamed."

"Ashamed of what?"

Her eyes shift to her lap. "I haven't been honest with you. I didn't think you were happy, but the truth is, I was the one that was miserable. I was projecting my problems onto you and once I realized that, I had to come here and tell you. I thought I could just leave a note and then put the ball in your court, so to speak."

She twists her hands in her lap, a move I'm familiar with. I put my hand over hers. "Do you want to talk about it?"

"Yes. No. I don't know. I wish we had talked sooner. I know you think my life is great, and our parents are proud, but nothing could be farther from the truth. I'm not as successful as you think. And our parents . . . Mom won't even talk to me right now."

Shock blows through me. "What? Why?"

"You know how critical they were when I started auditioning. 'It's not a real job.' " She says the last words in a dead-on impression of Mom, then rolls her eyes.

"Yeah, but you proved them wrong."

"So we thought. Mom still wanted me to have a fall-back plan, and she wasn't wrong, and that's why I applied to Stanford. But now, the truth is . . . I'm failing."

I blink and sit back on the couch. "What?"

"I sort of stopped going to classes and didn't tell anyone."

I stare at her in stunned silence.

"I know!" she wails, covering her face with her hands. "I couldn't face it. I didn't want to do it. I hated every second of every class. It's not what I want to do, and I only went because it was expected. Who gets accepted to Stanford and just, doesn't go? Me, that's who. And then when you were telling me about applying for the promotion at your work, I was upset and jealous and I feel like a failure."

"You're not a failure. You're . . . famous."

She snorts. "Except I'm never going to act again."

"Why not?"

"Malcom broke up with me."

"Oh, gosh. I'm sorry, Eloise, but what does Malcom

breaking up with you have to do with finding acting jobs?"

She lifts a brow. "He slept with Amanda Robbins."

"Isn't she . . . ?"

"She plays my sister on the show." She blows out a breath. "He had me written off. Then he spread stories about me acting erratically and that I'm a compulsive liar. It was a total smear campaign, so if I try tell the real story of how he cheated, he can push back by saying I'm a jealous liar." She wipes a tear from the corner of her eye. "I'm not going back when filming starts again. I don't know what I'm going to do. I failed school. I failed at acting. I have nothing left. And then I fought with you and it was mostly because I was trying to hide my own problems."

I grab a tissue from the side table and hand it to her, scooting closer on the couch. "You haven't failed. You can still try. You can find other acting jobs, no problem. You're a great actress."

She smiles weakly and takes the tissue, dabbing her eyes with it. "Thanks, but I don't know. The industry is brutal. I might have burned bridges."

"You only fail if you stop trying. You never know what's out there. Next week there will be some other scandal and people will forget. Besides, Hollywood loves a good comeback story."

She nods and we sit in comfortable silence for a few minutes, both processing. My sister, who I've been avoiding for months, all because I was ashamed and comparing myself to her, has been doing the same thing.

Even people who seem perfect on the outside have their own burdens to bear. We were both masking our true feelings and perceived failures, only to seem better than we were, or stronger. But is it stronger to hide and deny scary truths? Or is this, the unmasking and revealing of our personal disasters . . . is this the definition of bravery?

Is it because our parents are always putting pressure on us to be strong and smart and perfect? Or can we even blame them, when we're our own worst enemies?

All this time I've been trying to measure up to everyone else, when what I needed was to measure up to myself.

I blow out a breath. "I've been working at Blue Wave for four years and I'm still a junior associate. Most people are only junior associates for a year. I think I set some kind of record." I smile grimly, and then sigh and shut my eyes. "I avoided going to LA to see you because I was scared. I didn't want to disappoint you in front of your friends, make a fool of myself. After you moved out, I had no reason to keep trying. I let my anxiety get to the point where it limited my life. I've been lying to everyone, but not as much as I've been lying to myself. You were right about everything you said. And I got fired today, so there's that. We can be failures together."

She throws her arms around me, hugging me and shaking me in equal measure. "You're not a failure."

She pushes me back, hands on my shoulders. "You can get a new, better job. I know it."

I nod. "So basically, we were both jealous of each other, dealing with our own shame, and blaming each other for it."

She laughs. "I guess that's an accurate summary."

We smile at each other for a few seconds and it's like the weight of the Golden Gate Bridge has been lifted off my chest. "Let's get some good food. And wine. Can you stay for a little bit?"

She grins. "I can stay for a little while."

WE GET takeout from the Elephant Bar and sit in my living room on the floor, eating and talking about nothing and everything.

"Do you still make time for sewing?" Eloise asks, after we finish gorging ourselves on Korean beef tacos.

I take a deep breath. "If I show you something, do you promise not to laugh?"

Her brows lift. "Of course."

I stand up, getting items I've been saving in the magic closet, and toss the bundle in front of her on the floor.

"Jane." Eloise riffles through some of the finished work, holding up some of the gowns to inspect. "This is gorgeous. What did you make this for? Or who, I guess."

"Drag queens."

She stares at me, openmouthed. Then she grins. "No freaking way. That's amazing. Tell me how this happened."

I give her an extremely abbreviated version of events, having to omit the fact that I just met Hugo today. And it's not lying, for me it's been much longer than a day.

"Will you design a dress for me? Maybe not this extravagant. Maybe a classic design, but colorful instead of the requisite black. I hate black. I blame Mom. I mean, I don't know if I'm ever going to a red-carpet event again, but I'd like to think someday I will."

"You will. Eloise." I put my hand over hers. "I would love to make you a dress."

One she'll never actually get to wear until I can get Tuesday to happen. I shove the thought away. Dwelling won't help.

Eloise's phone trills with a call, the ringtone emanating from somewhere under the pile of fabric.

She delves into the stack and recovers it from under a purple strapless ballgown. She glances down at the screen and then meets my eyes with a wince. "It's Mom. Should I answer?"

"What? Is that even a real question? Do you hate good times and being happy?"

She smiles and shakes her head. "She's been calling me every day for the past week and I've been avoiding her." Her eyes search mine and then her brows lift. "Maybe we should talk to her together?"

My mouth twists. "Um, no?"

She shifts toward me. "Come on, Jane. We can come clean, get it over with, tell her the truth about our situations, as a team. We can support each other and maybe . . . maybe it will help."

We stare at each other, the phone continuing to ring between us.

"Do you not have voicemail set up?"

She rolls her eyes.

I bite my lip.

She's right. This is one more scary thing I need to face. And the only way out is through.

"Okay." I roll my hand. "Let's do it. Quick, like a Band-Aid."

She nods and answers the call, putting it on speaker and holding the phone between us.

"Oh, interesting." Mom's voice is a sarcastic whip, lashing the room before Eloise can even say hello. "You *can* answer the phone. I wasn't sure if it had been turned off for nonpayment or if you had forgotten how to use the device."

Eloise and I lock gazes. She rolls her eyes and I stifle a giggle. She's right. It is easier when I'm not the only one on the receiving end of a verbal flogging.

"Hello, Mother. It's nice to hear from you. How are you doing?"

"That's very cute, Eloise, but we need to talk about Stanford."

Cutting right to the chase, right where it bleeds.

Eloise swallows and I take her free hand. The

laughter in our eyes dies. Both of our palms are clammy, but it doesn't matter.

"I'm not going back. I'm dropping out." Her eyes widen at me, like she's surprised herself, and then her gaze dips to the phone.

The silence is deafening.

Eloise points at me, asking permission, and I nod.

"Jane is here with me too. She has something to say."

I take a breath and hold it for a second and then the words roll out. "I lost my job. I'm going to do something else, but I'm not sure what that is yet."

I've barely finished the sentence when she starts speaking. "I would say I'm surprised, but I'm not. You girls always did need a strong hand at your back to keep from quitting things. Good thing I'm here to keep you from making mistakes."

I blink. But *mistakes are how you learn.*

"I'll speak slowly so you both can understand." Her words are crisp and enunciated with care. "The solutions here are simple. Eloise, you will go back to Stanford and try again next term. Jane, you need to start looking for a decent job. I have some friends I can call."

Did she even hear what I said?

Eloise shakes her head. "No, Mom, I won't."

"And neither will I," I add. "You can't tell us what to do. We aren't puppets for you to manipulate however you think is best. We're your daughters. And we're adults. If you can't support our choices, even if they're mistakes, maybe we shouldn't talk anymore."

"I'm your mother. I only want what's best for you. Sometimes you can't see it, but that's what I'm here for. What I've always been here for since I brought you two into this world. You can't just throw away everything I've worked so hard to give you."

Here it is, the guilt trip. She gave us life and now we owe her all of it.

"Actually, we can do what we want. What you want isn't what's best. How many times have we told you we're miserable? But you're not listening. You're too busy directing. I can't speak for Eloise. For me, I would love to have a relationship with you, Mom, but it has to be a healthy one. And this isn't."

More silence. I wish I could see her reaction, but at the same time I'm glad I can't.

"I agree," Eloise says. After more silence, she adds, "Maybe we could do family therapy." She shrugs at me.

I shake my head back and forth so hard it'll fall off in a minute.

There's a click and silence on the other end. The call on Eloise's phone drops off the screen.

She stares down at the blank screen. "She . . . she hung up on us."

I nod. "I think it went well."

A small pause and then Eloise bursts out laughing, falling over onto her back on the floor.

Once the laughter subsides, Eloise wipes her eyes. "Do you think we did the right thing?"

"Having regrets already?"

She snorts. "Always."

"No regrets. Yes, she's our mother. Yes, she raised us but that doesn't give her the right to our sanity or happiness for all eternity."

She nods. "You're right. I'm glad we're at least in this together."

I smile. "Me too."

BY THE TIME ELOISE LEAVES, it's the middle of the night. I shut the door behind her, promising to call her tomorrow. Ha.

I get into bed and listen to Hugo's muffled sobs and contemplate everything.

What would make me happiest? How can I live as my truest self? Everything else is irrelevant. Which sounds selfish, but it's not. I can't help anyone else until I help myself.

I can't make my bosses like me.

I can't fix Hugo.

I can't live an entire relationship with Alex in the same twenty-four hours.

I can't force time to push on.

I had no idea what was happening with Eloise, and I can't fix her life for her now that I do.

And so. I have to let it go. Really let it go. Not like I did with Alex when we played hooky, a temporary reprieve from reality.

If I'm going to live the same day over and over with no control over the forward movement of time or anything else, then I'm damn well making sure it's the best day I can have.

I kept thinking if I held on tight, manipulated the things that happened around me, maneuvered the people around me, if I controlled *everything*, it would make me happy, but it doesn't work that way.

Look at Eloise. Or Mark. Or anyone, really. You can seem like you have everything, be perfect on the outside, and still be miserable on the inside. Perception is everything and nothing at all.

It's time to let go of what my parents want, what other people think I want, and figure out what I want. I can wear the expectations of everyone around me like a costume, like keeping it wrapped around me will give me happiness, but the opposite is true.

It's time to surrender. To let go of everything, including thinking I can do something to change this day. Instead of trying to control it, I should just enjoy it.

Chapter Twenty

OKAY, SO I DON'T TURN INTO SOME KIND OF SUPER calm yogi overnight who has no problems or nerves whatsoever. Letting go and enjoying the day doesn't mean anxiety is gone forever.

It also doesn't mean the day moves forward.

I stopped keeping track, but this Monday has been repeating for months. Five months? Six? Somewhere around there. It's a relatively small blip of time, but it may as well be an eternity.

But even though it feels like I'm living in a time without end, I am happier most days. Lighter. Freer.

Everyone has some anxiety. And it's not all a bad thing. Like feeling jittery before a performance or a job interview. Getting shaky talking to a crowd, or butter-flies before a first kiss. That's normal. That's healthy. That's your body understanding that you're doing something important.

When the acidic taste of panic rises in my throat for no good reason, I do my best. I know it won't last forever. I allow myself to feel it, recognize it for what it is, understand that it isn't the helpful kind of anxiety, and do my best to push through it. Just my best. Not perfection. It helps. I tell my brain the truth. There are no tigers hiding here. I'm not going to die. My body is overreacting to something that's not even real.

The difference is, I'm choosing not to dwell. I'm choosing not to let it take hold of me and limit my life. It's okay to feel it and then move on. I still get nervous and anxious, but it's not as much, and I'm getting better at fighting my way through it.

My days settle into something normal. As normal as it can be when you've been living the same day over and over (and over) again.

I still spend time with Hugo. Sometimes I hang out with Presley. And sometimes I go to Alex's show to support him. We still have the best conversations. Sometimes he asks me out and I get his kisses, sometimes I don't, and that's okay.

Sometimes when Eloise shows up, I bring her with me to drinks with the queens and she loves them as much as I do.

And most importantly, I stop overthinking and focus on what I can actually do to help Hugo.

I can't get him to not cry, and that's not on me. Maybe stopping the crying completely shouldn't have been the goal in the first place.

Instead, when the crying starts, I stop thinking of

Hugo as a problem to be solved, get out of bed, and go over and knock.

The door swings open. He's in the red dress, no wig, black lines of watery mascara trailing down his cheeks. My heart aches for him.

"Can I offer you solutions or comfort? Or do you want me to leave you alone?"

He blinks and then considers for a moment before responding. "Will you sit with me?"

"Of course."

I follow him to the couch, his large frame dwarfing the love seat. I drop down next to him and wait.

It's quiet, maybe a little awkward, but it's okay. The silence isn't making me too twitchy. Maybe it's because I've spent a lot of time with Hugo, or maybe it's because I know he's upset and he asked me to sit with him, and I'm doing what he wants.

He's still crying, his tears now silent.

After a minute, he leans into me, our shoulders touching.

And we sit, together.

I can't fix him. But I can be here for him. That's the only thing I have to offer, and so I give what I can and let the rest go.

ONE MORNING AFTER GETTING FIRED—AGAIN—I treat myself to a nice brunch at MKT Restaurant inside the Four Seasons, with extra mimosas, because, why not?

On my way home to take a nap before meeting Hugo, I'm gazing out the window of the cab, only a few blocks from home, when we pass the sign.

"It's back." The words explode from my mouth in a near yell.

"What?" Startled, the cab driver glares at me in the rearview.

"Can you pull over here, please?"

He parks. I pay him and jump out of the car, racing back down the block to the Druid's Stone.

I push on the door and it swings open.

"You're back!" I exclaim to . . . no one. Nothing's changed. Same old giant cash register, same cluttered shelves, same cuckoo clock in the corner.

Same teenage girl just waiting to pop up when I least expect it, I'm sure.

I meander around for a minute, but she doesn't appear.

I yawn. The mimosas made me sleepy. There's nowhere to sit in here, so I head down the hallway to the garden in the back.

Still no sign of my psychic friend, so I sit on the bench and lean back, closing my eyes and taking a deep breath.

It's nice and quiet, just the soothing tumble of water through the fountain in the corner.

I open my eyes and am unsurprised that someone is

sitting next to me, sitting way too close, even though I didn't hear her sit down.

"Hello," I say.

She smiles. "I love this garden."

"Me too. It's peaceful."

She nods and we sit together, unmoving, unspeaking for long minutes. Time passes. I'm not sure how long, but it doesn't really matter.

"The only way through is to love, Jane."

I lift my brows, surprised she spoke first. "Yeah, you've mentioned that."

She nods.

My mind wanders. I gaze at the fountain, watching the water fall into the pond.

The only way through is to love. That's what she said the first time I came here. No. She said, *the only way through is to love, Jane.*

The same thing she said just now.

Kind of weird she said it again—and it doesn't work, by the way, I mean I love Alex, and yet I'm still here and maybe I should mention to her that she is way off. But—

Wait.

Something in my chest twists and wrenches. I suck in a sharp breath.

No. *No.* I was wrong. I heard it wrong.

She isn't telling me the only way through is for me to love someone, or something, else.

That's what I heard, but it's not what she said.

Time is outside. Happiness is inside.

Bee said something similar. It has to come from in here. In me.

What she said was the only way through is to love *Jane*.

There's no comma.

I put the comma there.

Lightheaded, I slump on the bench, the realization washing over me in a wave, the truth of it sinking into my bones and settling with the *rightness* of it.

She didn't say, *Jane, the only way through is to love,* she said I need *to love Jane.*

Me. I need to love *myself.* Accept myself, exactly as I am, warts and all.

I blink back tears. Holy hell, that's deep.

Giddiness pulses through me. I want to hoot at the sky, but at the same time I'm struck silent, immobile, reeling with emotions. Happiness that I know what I need to work on next, satisfaction that I figured it out, and fear that I won't be able to do something so simple and yet so essential. Why is it so hard to love myself?

"Isn't it a beautiful day?" my teenage best friend says. Her head tilts back, eyes shut, a small smile on her face.

I grin up at the desolate fog. "It sure as shit is."

Chapter Twenty-One

"I REALLY LOVE YOUR SHIRT," STACEY SAYS. "IS THAT new?"

"It is." I grin. "I made it."

"Really?" One of Stacey's brows quirk up.

The blouse is a bright teal, paired with black pants that have matching teal seams. I did my makeup and hair the way Dolly taught me, taking extra time, which means I showed up even later than normal, but I'm late every day and it never makes a difference. I simply don't care anymore. I realize now that it doesn't matter, so why let it stress me out? I'm just hurting me. No one else gives a shit.

"We're ready when you are," Blade says.

"Right so . . ." I stare down at the papers in my hands.

What am I doing? Why am I doing this to myself? Is this really what I want? Am I putting myself through this every day because I want to keep working here, or am I doing it because I want to prove to them I can?

Blade motions with a hand. "Being the focus of attention is something you'll have to get used to for the position you want. It's best to get started."

But do I want this position? Is it even about me, or is it about what people think about me? "Actually," I shake my head, "no."

"No?" Blade and Drew exchange a glance. This time, it's not commiserating looks of irritation aimed in my general direction. They're surprised. Blade's brows are nearly to his hairline and Drew . . . well, he still looks pretty stern and serious, actually.

"Yeah, no. I'm not going to do this. I quit."

They continue to exchange looks, a silent message passing between the three of them. Something I'm used to, but this time it's . . . different. Stacey is smiling. Drew's lips are pursed, a small groove between his brows. Blade is frowning, but that's how he always looks.

"I get that I don't fit in, okay? I know it. And frankly, I don't care. So." I shrug. "Have a nice day." I leave, walking away, leaving them in the room gaping after me. I'm grinning so big my cheeks hurt. I finally freaking did it.

I totally nailed my pitch. I laugh out loud, giddy. That was fun. And, even better, I can quit again tomorrow if I want.

But the euphoria is short lived.

"Hey. Jane. Come with me." Mark grabs my hand.

I tug my fingers from his grasp. "Mark. Stop."

He stills, watching me with wide eyes.

"I'm not sleeping with you, okay?"

His eyes grow impossibly larger. "What?"

"Listen. It's over. And in the future, you should probably be clear with whoever you want to mess around with that it's meaningless sex and nothing serious. It's not fair to give people the wrong idea. I'm human too. I have wants and needs, and I need more than a quick bang in a closet."

His mouth hangs open, eyes so wide they might pop out of his skull.

"Look. I get it. You want an escape, a good time, all that, and that's fine. You do you. But if you're not up front about your intentions, people get hurt. And maybe all of that could have been prevented with one honest conversation. Is that so much to ask?"

His mouth opens and closes like a fish. "Um, I, you, I don't know—"

"Mark. It's fine." I pat him on the shoulder. "It's okay to grieve."

"Grieve? Who said anything about—"

"And it's okay to feel guilty. It's okay to feel however you feel, but don't lead other people on. Maybe talk to someone about it. Oh, here." I reach into my briefcase for the card I've been carrying to work every day—and having to recreate every day. "It's a list of grief counselors. Think about it. Okay?"

I walk away, and I don't look back.

"How did it go?" Presley stops me in the communal area.

"Fantastic. I quit."

A startled laugh bubbles out of her. "That's fantastic?"

"Oh yeah."

"Wow. I have no idea what to say. Congratulations?"

"That works. Hey, want to celebrate later? I'm going to watch Alex's band play at the Saloon. I'll be there around eight. You should come."

A crease forms between her brows. "Alex? Alex Chambers, our client Alex?"

"The very one." I grin. "Not my client though. Not anymore."

She stares at me, eyes narrowed. "You sure you want a tagalong to that?"

"You wouldn't be tagging along. I'm bringing other friends. You could meet them, since you're new in town. Unless you don't want to?"

She blinks. "Oh, no. I mean, yes, I absolutely would love to come. That would be great." She beams at me.

"Great. I gotta run. I'll see you later."

Outside, footsteps slap the pavement behind me.

"Hey, Jane. You okay?"

I spin around. "I'm great. How are you?"

He blinks, baffled.

I smile. He's so adorable when he's confused.

He rubs the back of his neck. "Are you leaving? You never take a day off."

"I'm not taking a day off. I quit. I don't work here anymore."

His mouth pops open. "Oh. Okay. And this is a good thing, it seems?"

"It's great. I'm going to design clothes."

He barks out a laugh. "That is . . . incredibly amazing."

I nod. "Yeah. I think so too."

We're both smiling, looking at each other, and then Alex shoves his hands in his pockets and his gaze drops to the ground between us.

He takes a breath and meets my eyes. "Hey, listen, I'm in a band. We have a gig tonight. I mean, it's not a big thing, we're the opening act and it's at the Saloon, but you should come. I'll buy you a drink. To celebrate, I guess."

"I'll be there."

We grin at each other like two idiots for a few long seconds, and I hold on to this moment, keeping it in my heart like a prayer. "Oh." I glance down at my watch. Right. I have places to be. "I gotta run. Hugo needs me. But I'll see you later, for sure." On a whim, I lean up and kiss him on the cheek. Then I turn to leave, but he stops me with a hand on my arm.

"Wait, Jane." His eyes devour me, and then a crease forms between his brows. "Who is Hugo?"

"A friend. He's got an audition for a drag show and his partner is going to bail. I have to bring him a costume."

His head tilts and one side of his mouth tips up.

"What is with you today? You seem so different." He rubs his chin. "No. That's not right, you still seem like yourself, but—"

"I'm still me. I'm just more me."

He nods slowly. "Right."

I back away. I need to get back. "I'll see you later."

"Yeah, see you," he calls out, but I'm already running to the pay phone.

～

"ELOISE?"

I make it to my building just in time. I had to rush back to Emeryville after watching Dolly audition and hanging out with the queens and inviting them to Alex's show later.

Eloise is walking out the front entrance, her gaze is lowered, and she's deep in thought so when I say her name, she startles and looks up.

"Oh, hey." She gives me a tremulous smile, her eyes darting to the ground before landing on my face. "I thought you were at work and I left a note and I—"

"It's okay. Listen, I want to apologize. I've been terrible and you didn't deserve it. Can you come upstairs so we can talk?"

Her mouth opens and closes. "Yes. Yes, of course."

We go upstairs and have our conversation and after that's done, again, I give her the dress I've been working on for a while now. Of course, she doesn't know that.

"Here. I made this for you." I hand her the dress.

It's a simple design, strapless, tight around the bust, and the skirt is an asymmetrical ruffle. But the colors are vibrant, varying shades of red and purple and white.

"Jane, it's gorgeous. When did you make this?" She takes it into my room to hold it up in front of the mirror.

"Oh you know." I shrug, leaning against the doorframe while she examines it. "I had some spare time and I've been playing around."

"Playing around?" She spins to face me, her eyes wide. "This is incredible."

"Good. I'm glad you approve." I also knew she would approve since we discussed the design and I measured her for it a week ago, but she doesn't remember that. I glance at the clock. "Oh we should get ready. They'll be waiting for us."

"Who's waiting for us?"

"My friends." I grin. "C'mon. Let's go out."

"WE SHOULD FIND HARRY, cut off his balls, throw them in the bay, dump him off at Alcatraz, and let the birds eat him." Queen Bee lifts her glass like she's toasting instead of roasting.

"That's seems maybe a little excessive?" Eloise says, but she raises her glass to Bee's with a smile.

"Baby, morally gray is my favorite color."

Presley bursts out laughing.

We snagged a table at the Saloon for Alex's show,

me, Bee, Fifi, Dolly, and Eloise. Presley showed up shortly after we arrived, and we've all been enjoying ourselves ever since.

Instead of the mild clapping and chuckles that normally accompany Alex and Leon's comedy show, we've been tearing it up with cheers and laughter, and when Dolly laughs, she is *loud*.

Their energy ramps up the whole half-full room until it's an exuberant celebration of humor.

"Hey. You made it. And you brought friends." After the set ends, Alex stops next to me at the table.

"Hey! Yes, I did. Everyone, everyone?" I have to clap my hands to get their attention.

Queen Bee is giving Eloise red-carpet makeup tips, Dolly is interjecting her opinions, and Presley is arguing with Bee about lash extensions.

I introduce Alex to the queens and to my sister.

"Want to sit? We saved you a seat."

"Yeah. Sure."

He sits and immediately gets roped into an argument about the best place to eat in Oakland.

Conversation hums around me, mingled with periodic bursts of laughter. I sit back and enjoy, contributing occasionally, but mostly breathing in the moments. Delighting in the fact that I'm surrounded by people who are kind and open and accepting and full of joy just existing with each other. People I love.

Leon comes over at some point, and the merriment increases. Then Leon ends up in Fifi's lap, and the volume goes up another notch. Time flies by. I blink and Eloise is hugging everyone goodbye.

"You're leaving?"

"Yeah. It's midnight and I've got to get back to Palo Alto. I'll call you, okay?"

"My phone's broken. I'll call you once I get it fixed."

And I'll see you tomorrow anyway, I add in my head.

Later, we get Bee and Fifi off in a cab, and then Alex drives Dolly and me home. This time, I don't fall asleep, and Alex doesn't idle in front of the building. He shuts off his truck and walks Dolly and me up to our floor.

After Dolly disappears into her place, Alex stops with me outside my apartment.

I lean back against my door and face him. "Thanks for giving us a ride."

His hands are in his pockets. "Thanks for coming to my show."

"It was a lot of fun."

"So—"

"I'll see you tomorrow."

I want him to come in, of course, but I don't want to pressure him and I know how this ends. Plus, I have to check on Dolly.

But Alex isn't moving.

I lift my brows at him.

"You're not going inside? I was sort of waiting for you to go in so I could do that thing where I pine outside your door like a smitten fool."

I laugh. "That sounds like an amazing time for you, but . . ." I consider what to tell him and settle on the truth. I'm not giving away any of Dolly's secrets. "I'm probably going to check on Dolly."

Of course Alex, being himself, is concerned. "Is she okay? Is there something I can do?"

I shrug. "Sometimes she just needs someone to sit with her."

He nods, getting it. "Can I help?"

Chapter Twenty-Two

WAKEFULNESS WEAVES ITS FINGERS THROUGH MY SLEEPY mind. I roll over, pulling a pillow over my head in anticipation of drowning out the thumping music.

I can't wait to do this day all over again. Maybe I can push Alex for some heavy petting or something. He's too damn chivalrous.

Wait.

I remove the pillow from over my head.

There's no music. No thumping. No sprinkle me.

I sit up in bed. Why is the music gone? I don't oversleep. I don't sleep through E-40. I don't wake up before it starts. Not ever.

What if I've gone deaf? Is that possible?! I pick up the lamp on my side table and chuck it on the floor.

It doesn't shatter, it thumps to the ground. But it does make a noise, and I can hear it. Not deaf.

I pick up my phone. It's still dead.

Knock knock knock.

That's the same. Sort of. Is it louder, or does it seem louder because there's no music overpowering . . . ?

I open the door.

Alex.

I blink at him, my mouth agape.

Alex is standing at my doorstep, his arms full of brown Trader Joe's grocery bags. "I got bagels and coffee and some fresh fruit and stuff." He breezes past me.

I stare into the hallway outside my door. I can't move. I'm a statue of shock.

I can't—I can't believe it. It's different. It's really different.

My whole body flashes hot and cold. I can't come to grips with this. After all this time, after all these days, days that I had gotten used to living, didn't expect to change, had let go of wanting to change and . . . now it's tomorrow.

"I also got some creamer and sugar. Real sugar and the fake sugar and vegan sugar." He's in my kitchen, pulling stuff out of the bags and setting them on the counter. "I wasn't sure what you preferred." He looks up.

Our eyes lock.

I stare at him. "You're here."

"Yeah. Sorry." He grimaces and rubs the back of his neck. "I woke up early. Not because your couch is super uncomfortable or anything, but because it's literally the worst thing I've ever slept on."

A startled laugh escapes me.

One corner of his mouth tips up in a lopsided grin. "Then I couldn't leave without locking your door, since I don't want you to get murdered or anything, but then I couldn't get back in and suffice it to say, it wasn't well thought out." He holds up a package of instant coffee. "I brought back caffeine." His sheepish smile is the cutest thing I've seen on a Tuesday, ever.

I don't know if I should laugh or cry or some combination of the two. I'm still standing in the open doorway.

I shut the door and take a few steps into the kitchen. I have to make sure. "What day is this?"

He puts bagels on the counter and cream cheese, then pulls more items out of the bags, fruit, milk, yogurt, loading up my fridge and freezer. Did he do all my shopping for me?

"I think it's the eighth." He stops and looks at me. His smile falters. I can't even imagine what my face looks like right now. White with shock? Stunned and blank? Stupefied and absurd?

"Why?" A crease forms between his brows. "Are you okay?"

No. No, I'm not okay. I mean, I am okay. I'm better than okay. Is there a word to describe what it feels like to be exactly where you want to be, the world suddenly open before you with an actual future?

"It's Tuesday." I step closer to him.

He nods slowly. "Yes."

I slide my hands up to his neck, to the back of his head. He leans down.

And then we're kissing. Our first kiss.

Well, his first kiss with me, my first kiss with him on a Tuesday.

I get lost in him, in us.

He pulls back, resting his forehead against mine. "Do you not like bagels? We could go out somewhere for breakfast."

"You bought me a week's worth of food."

He shrugs. "You literally had nothing but condiments. How do you live?"

I'm not concerned about food right now. "It's Tuesday."

"Yes. I think we've covered that. I might be wrong. Your lips have scrambled my brain a little." He smiles and kisses me again.

This time I pull back. "Wait, how did we get here?"

"Well, first you kissed me. Then I kissed you, and now—"

I giggle. "No, I mean last night. I don't remember leaving Dolly's."

"Oh, you both fell asleep on her couch. It was very cute, and the first time I've ever thought having a woman I like fall asleep next to someone else is precious, but then you woke up, pretty groggy and out of it, and we came back here."

I frown, trying to recall the prior evening. "I don't remember any of that."

"You zombie walked into your room, and I crashed

on the devil couch." His eyes search my face and then he adds, "Maybe I shouldn't have stayed? Was that presumptuous? I was a little worried because you seemed like you were sleep walking, and you said something about naked lightsabers, which was really weird actually, because Leon and I had this experience one night . . . well, we don't really talk about it. So it was a weird coincidence."

Zombie just about describes the state of my mind at this very moment. How is this possible?

Alex misconstrues my continued silence, and probably bizarre facial expressions. "Are you sure you're all right? Oh." His face clears. "Is it the job? You were so calm about it yesterday, but maybe now it's catching up? Have you decided what you're going to do next?"

I laugh, a little hysterical. Am I upset? No. Do I think I might cry anyway? Yes.

"I'm not upset. I mean, I don't know what I'm going to do with the rest of my life, which is scary but also freeing somehow. Maybe I'll get a new job somewhere and design things on the side. Maybe I'll make a go of design full-time." I move back into him, wanting to feel the warm strength of him against me. I put my hands on his shoulders. "Maybe I'll take over the world. I don't know. I do know what I'm doing tonight."

His brows lift. "Tonight?"

I nod. "Dinner. We're going out to dinner."

"Right. Dinner." His hands move to my hips and squeeze. "Do you think we could have breakfast first though? I'm starving. But dinner later is cool too. I do think I asked you out last night. Or I meant to."

I slide my fingers up to where his shoulder meets his neck and rub my thumbs over the tendons there. "Or we could stay in tonight."

His smile is smooth and warm. He leans his forehead against mine. "We could."

Then he leans in, kissing my bottom lip, and we lose ourselves in discovery. Rediscovery.

When we part again, we're both breathing heavily.

"Should we check on your neighbor?" Alex asks. "She was sleeping when we left last night, but maybe we should make sure everything is okay. Maybe we can share some breakfast."

I nod. "Yes. Let's do that. You did buy enough food for this whole floor."

He laughs. "And then you can tell me your plan to take over the world."

I grin and tap him on the shoulder. "Only if you tell me the whole naked lightsaber story."

He laughs. "How did you—?"

I pull him closer. "Tomorrow." I want more kissing first. "I'll tell you all about it tomorrow."

THE END

Go here to sign up for the newsletter! www. authormaryframe.com

Mary Frame is a full-time mother and wife with a full-time job. She has no idea how she manages to write novels except that it helps being a dedicated introvert. She doesn't enjoy writing about herself in third person, but she does enjoy reading, writing, dancing, and damaging the eardrums of her coworkers when she randomly decides to sing to them. She lives in Reno, Nevada, with her husband, two children, and a border collie named Stella.

She LOVES hearing from readers and will not only respond but likely begin stalking them while tossing out hearts and flowers and rainbows! If that doesn't creep you out, email her at:

maryframeauthor@gmail.com

CPSIA information can be obtained
at www.ICGtesting.com
Printed in the USA
LVHW052342011121
702138LV00005B/927

9 781954 372122